FITEVER!

The Upcoming Marriage of
The Whiny Quinie

D0727681

Published 2016 by Fitever Publishing,
27 Lauriston Street, Edinburgh, UK, EH3 9DQ,

Copyright © Robin Smith

The right of Robin Smith to be identified as the author
of this work has been asserted by him in accordance
with the Copyright, Designs and Patents Act, 1988.

ISBN 978-1-904684-32-9

Dedications

This book is dedicated to my daughters, the friends I've made in Aberdeen since I returned and, of course, Angela, without whom Fitever! would never have been thought of.

Contents

Birdsong

It sounded like birdsong. At least, in Pat's head it did. He remembered noticing it for the first time 25 years ago, when he slept on a bench at the harbour in Tarbert, Argyll, in 1989. And later, wherever he was in the world with the army, Pat loved to hear the first morning birdsong. As a musician, Pat had appreciated any music but natural music had a purity, something that offered the previous bloody day some sort of redemption.

Pat didn't know which was loudest; the ringing in his head – or the ringing of the phone.

"Who's calling at this hour, for crying out loud?!" It was midday.

Pat staggered out of bed, eyes still closed and in denial that the day had started. He stumbled over to the mantelpiece, inadvertently kicking over a can of something smelling beer-like. His eyes still closed, he searched with his hands on the mantelpiece, vaguely fumbling in the direction of the ringing. He knocked over a large glass and it smashed against the fireplace. Its contents also smelled beer-like. Damn, he thought. He'd have to open his eyes!

Eventually he found the phone, picked it up, muttering into the mouthpiece, "Aye. Whit is it." There was no reply. He'd taken too long to answer, so it had just hung up.

A quieter ringing and vibrating started coming from the other side of the room, where his sofa bed was, where he'd just walked over from. It was his mobile going off in his jacket pocket. He groaned. But, his eyes were open now so the return journey was less perilous than the blind tumble to the mantelpiece. Now he could see the obstacles and the mystery of why everything seemed beer-smelling was solved. The carpet was littered with empty cans, and a spilled-over chilli sauce carton.

"Pakora!" He remembered now. "Breakfast."

However, it was soon apparent that he'd eaten 'breakfast' before he'd went to bed. He scrunched up the empty brown paper bag that has once held this culinary delight and threw it in the bin.

"Bloody hell. Not even close. I'm worse than Scotty Vernon. I need to get a grip."

Unless you were one of the few Aberdeen fans in Glasgow, where Pat was waking up, you wouldn't ever know who Scott Vernon was. Suffice to say that there was once a Twitter account set up under the name @HasVernonScoredYet. While an honest and decent player, Vernon's goals were a little too infrequent for some Dons fans liking.

Pat got to his jacket just as the phone stopped ringing. He took it out the pocket and checked the number. His eyes staggered around just as his legs had done before. They eventually focused.

"01224 number? That's … Aberdeen."

He sat down beside his portable record player. Pat hated the radio. The talking on it pissed him off because everything they said on it was "propaganda". And the music! Jesus, was that really music? What the hell. It jangled him up every time. So, one of the few possession that followed him out the army was his portable record player. He put on *The Doors, LA Woman* LP. *The Changling* started. Pat wondered how *Lipps & Co* had gotten away with using the exact same intro for *Funky Town* years later. Then Jim Morrison started singing.

Ah, that was better. It was like an alcoholic's first drink of the morning. Now the day had actually started.

Pat turned up the record player to full. Bizarrely it soothed the pounding in his head. He picked up a can of beer, shook it to feel if there were any contents left in it. He felt the mini waves roll around in the tin. "Boost." And he drank the contents. A bit flat, but, hey, who was choosey? Besides, it was like he was on leave, he told himself. In reality, he was on permanent leave. He'd left the army with no job or home to go to. No preparation for this mission, the mission being to live the rest of his life.

Pat finished the can, and threw it up in the air, then as it fell down he kicked it in the direction of the bin. It landed right in. "Yass! Scotty Vernon! One nil!"

Pat sat down again at the small table for one in the city centre flat his best friend, Willie, had lent him while he was away on business. He'd only been out the army a month but it felt like a lifetime ago already. 25 years. His mind started drifting and suddenly instances of comradeship, of fun, of danger, of horror, would all flit across his mind like they were happening right here, right now, such was their intensity. Pat opened and shut his eyes a few times just to make sure they weren't.

Oh well. Time for the new morning routine. Pat picked up his jeans. They'd been crumpled in a heap. He took perverse joy not folding a damn thing any more. He'd been neat and tidy for quarter of a century and it hadn't exactly done him wonders like they'd once said it would. Pat looked for the note book that had become essential for his new life. He noted important things in it, like who he was meeting that day, if anybody. A whole bunch of people seemed to have been shoved his way in order to help him "adjust". The only

3

thing they taught him was that they should be avoided at all costs.

In his notebook a crunched up bit of paper fell out. It had been ripped from a lined page. It had a phone number on it. The words "call me" were written on it. Pat had no idea who this was. Should he ring it? What if it was someone he'd forgotten to meet? It embarrassed him, forgetting things. His memory seemed to have deteriorated over the last month.

So, Pat rang the number, wiping the traces of beer from his lips and clearing his throat. Someone answered.

"Well, hello, Pat! I'm so pleased! Thanks for calling!"

Flip. It all came back to him. It was someone called Debbie who he'd never met before last night. He looked around the room. An empty bottle of wine on the window sill gave it away. He never drank wine. Someone else must have been here.

"I knew you'd remember!"

Pat hung up the phone, blocked the number and took the bit of paper back into his hands. Rip. Zip. Bin. End of correspondence. The paper was still fluttering into the bin when Pat took his mobile back out his pocket and sat hunched in the chair, holding the phone in both hands. He stared at the screen. "Aberdeen?" he muttered questioningly.

Aberdeen

Dorothy put the phone hurriedly back into her pocket as her daughter, Kylie, came barging into her bedroom. Kylie came barging into everywhere. That was her style.

"So, ma, fa are you sneaking aff to your room to call? Have you got a trap?" Kylie laughed.

A "trap" was an Aberdonian expression for a snog and/or a snogger. It'd been a long time since her mother had had a trap.

"No, sweetheart, just a bit of business. So, are you all ready for the Wedding Fair?"

"Aye, aye. Ma, are you gan oot like that?"

"Like what?"

"In your pyjamas? "

"This is a leisure suit!"

"Well, Ma, you're no gan in your leisure suit. Get changed. I'll tell Dod to wait a bitty before he picks us up."

"I thought he wasn't coming."

"Aye, so did he. He's coming all right, da worry aboot that!"

"Are you sure Dod is marrying you voluntarily?" said Dorothy, smiling and getting changed. Everyone knew there was no point in arguing with Kylie. She wasn't called The Whiny Quinie for nothing.

"Like it matters, Ma."

Big Dod, a rugby-playing farmland boy from Echt, was much admired by all for the way he effortlessly took his life-direction from Kylie, his betrothed. Fair-haired and fair-natured, he was the perfect antidote to the redheaded firestorm that was Kylie.

Kylie came downstairs into the kitchen. She was rounding up the posse. Yes, it was only she and Dod who were getting married, but Kylie liked an audience. So they were all coming to the Wedding Fair if they liked it or not. Everybody on Facebook, Twitter, Instagram, virtually the whole world, knew of Kylie's every move in life.

"Granda. We're leaving in 15 minutes. Are you ready?"

"Why are we leaving in 15 minutes? The bloody thing doesn't start till 10am!"

"Fitever, Granda!"

Kylie's Granda was, in the permanent absence of Kylie's father, the undisputed patriarch of the tribe. Even the Summerhill Mob, a collection of aunts, uncles and cousins of all ages, deferred to Kylie's Granda. Despite his gruff manner, he had their interests at heart, most of the time, even after he'd worked out that they all called him *Grumphy*.

"It only takes hauf an oor to get there, quinie."

"Traffic, Granda, traffic!"

"On a Sunday? At 9 am? Fit's happened that I've missed? Is the circus coming to toon? Has there been an alien landing? Fit the f*** are we rushing oor breakfast for? Jeez, I'm just up!"

"Now, Georgie, just wheesh and get ready. We all ken you'll be hours in the cludgie," said his wife, universally known as Mither.

"It's nae my fault!"

"Granda, we want to be first there. Beat the queues. It's all about preparation."

"Aye, I suppose the quicker we're there, the quicker we can get back for the Don's game."

"Fit! The Don's game! Kick off isn't until 12.30!"

"Preparation, quinie, preparation."

"Aye, aye, you mean 'the pub' mair like."

"If that's no preparation for the torture The Dons put us through, I da ken fit is."

"Fitever! Noo, get ready!"

Grumphy looked to the ceiling and groaned. "Well, she disnae get a that fae me!" He was looking at Mither as he said it – not a good move if a wee bit of peace was what he was hoping for.

"Aye, well, we'll no get intae fit she gets fae you, then."

Grumphy looked to the side with a faintly appalled expression on his face, as if he was in a TV show and grimacing at the camera for comic effect. Then he looked back at his plate. "Farewell, bonnie breakfast, I kent you well."

"Very touching. But dinna worry, you can ging to the toilet and get reacquainted with it ASAP," said Mither as if her comment was revenge for the look Grumphy thought he'd gotten away with. "15 minutes and counting."

That Big Lump Of Dod

Dod parked outside Kyle's Esslemont Terrace flat, where she lived with her mum and grandparents. He called her.

"Everybody ready, Kyle?"

"No, they're nae. You're early."

"Eh? You said 9.15am?"

"That's no like you to actually listen to fit I said. Anyway, I just texted you to make it 15 minutes later. Ma's changing out her so-called leisure suit into something less humiliating."

"Quine, I canna leave the car here. You ken fit the wardens are like round here."

"Dod! Fit did I say about the wardens?"

Oh shit, thought Dod. Here comes the YOU DON'T LISTEN TO ME! speech again.

"I ken fit you're thinking. But it's not *my* fault," said Kylie.

"Fit's not?"

"That you don't listen to me!"

"I didn't say it was your fault!"

"You thought it though."

She's good, Dod thought to himself. Bloody good.

"Noo, back to the wardens. Fit day is it?"

"Sunday." Dod knew some arrow from somewhere was going to hit him. These questions were just Kylie dragging back the bow, for maximum impact. He was in her sights. No point in running. There was no escaping. She was a crack shot. Just brace himself and get it over with.

"And fa doesn't come oot on Sundays until 1pm?"

"Traffic Wardens," said Dod, through gritted teeth."

"So, fit are you spickin' aboot it, min? Get in here and get a cuppy while we wait. Grumphy's in the bog."

Dod parked the car illegally and sure, if someone wanted to complain, he'd put them right through to Kylie. Then he'd get the popcorn out and watch.

Mither opened the door. "Dod, you look fantastic. You'll put us all to shame. Very handsome, young man."

"Thanks, Mrs B."

Grumphy entered the hallway from the bathroom, doing up his belt as he looked at Dod. "Dod, it's only the Wedding Fair today, no the flipping wedding."

"Thanks Grumphy – err – I mean Mr Buchan."

Grumphy momentarily stopped fixing his belt, as if to chide Dod for calling him Grumphy. But, he was philosophical when it suited him, so he let it go and belted up, pointing to the bathroom. "I wouldnae ging in there for a whilie just yet."

Mither's eyes rolled. "Come away in, Dod. Kylie's got a cuppy for you. How do you take it again?"

"However she makes it," laughed Dod. He could hear Grumphy laughing too.

As Dod sat down with his cup of tea, Grumphy pushed some plates out the way and got his AA map of Aberdeen out and rolled it over the table, like a general in his element. "Now, young Dod, here's the operational route. I've marked here …"

"Fit are you daein', Granda?"

Grumphy did his off-camera look again, as he always did when exasperation took hold. Then he looked back at Kylie, saying, "Dod's only fae Echt. How is he meant to ken the best route? And apparently there's a race against time involved."

"Dinna exaggerate, Granda. And put that map awa. It's an affa mess on the table. Besides, Dod's got Sat Nav noo."

"Sat Nav? On a tractor? Noo, that's clever."

Dod laughed. "I left the tractor at home today, Mr Buchan."

Call Back

Glasgow

It'd been years since Pat had been in Aberdeen. He'd been born there, and indeed had supported the Dons all his life, despite growing up in Glasgow. He'd eventually gotten a job in Aberdeen in 1986. He'd moved up there on the same day Fergie left The Dons for Manchester United, earning him the nickname, *Jonah,* among Dons-supporting pals.

"Job" was perhaps an exaggeration. He was singing in bars. See, before Pat became all sensible and joined the army, he was en route to becoming a rock star. He'd certainly mastered the requirements. He drank like a fish, smoked strange ciggies, and rebelled against all authority, which all helped him lose the few paying gigs he was getting. Anyway, he was getting tired waiting in the queue to become famous.

To make ends meet he got a sales job, selling book club membership door to door. His colleagues there had all been in the same queue. Some were aspiring writers, comedians, singers, musicians, drinkers. As well as a great sense of their own artistic talent they all shared a great refusal to becoming arsed about anything. This motley crew smoked and drank their way through the week, defying gravity along the way by somehow remaining standing and, in some cases, breathing.

Then Pat, living in Bervie, met an "affa bonnie quine" as his colleagues described her. She, from Aberdeen, was going to 'fix' him. She saw something he'd lost in himself. A

11

decency, a kindness, a strength and she was going to damn well bring all that out in him. But Pat didn't take kindly to his better-self being rescued from the loch of alcohol he'd immersed it in. Dramas and conflicts resulted, far too many to recount.

One day Pat had woken up, in every sense, and decided being normal and square was not perhaps the living hell as he'd once imagined it to be. It was certainly less of a living hell than drinking his wages before they were paid. Even his long-indulging, subbing local publican, Gordon, lost patience. So when Pat had strolled in with some work mates one night and ordered "three pints – and change of £30", he heard Gordon say "no" for the first time.

This was before the days of mobile phones so one day Pat had got the bus from Bervie to Aberdeen, then ran from Union Street to Esslemont Terrace in Rosemount so he could tell his very patient Blonde, Dorothy, that he'd seen the light, that he was going to change, and that he loved her. Had he done this even a day before she might have still been there. But, as Pat found out when Dorothy's mother answered the door, she'd gone to stay with her aunt in Tarbert on the west coast. She might as well have gone to the moon. Pat begged Dorothy's mum for a number, or even an address. But she'd just asked him to leave her daughter alone.

Fast forward to three days later and Pat, having just got off a bus in Tarbert, was walking around asking complete strangers if they knew of a Dorothy from Aberdeen. If they knew they weren't telling. Soaked by the west coast summer rain, he drank coke in a dank pub as he figured what to do next. Here he was, all well-dressed and sensible, sober even, and no one to show his new-found best-self to. He slept on a bench by the harbour, his newly-bought suit (bought with money borrowed from Gordon the publican) being little use against the cold despite it being June 1989. In the morning he called into the few places he hadn't before, all to no avail. Reluctantly, he got the bus to Glasgow, stayed with old friends, who called him boring because he refused drink beer and smoke hash, customary hospitality in that part of Shawlands in Glasgow's south side.

So, Pat joined the army, where he stayed, tee-total and drug-free, for most of the next 25 years. He hadn't even gone back to Bervie to pick up his things, not even his vinyl record collection, which was gradually sold by his house-mates, along with some tables, chairs and some wall fittings, for drink money. His closest Bervie pal, Willie, followed instructions to sell his guitar and amplifier and give the proceeds to Gordon the publican.

Pat had felt born again in Gütersloh, West Germany. Sadness at losing the love of his life was soon replaced with gratitude to her. Turned out that his better-self, which Dorothy has discovered inside him, had found a home after all. The army became his mammy and daddy, his brother and sister, the new love of his life.

But later Pat found out the army's love was conditional and didn't extend to even favoured sons who threw a series of boxer-quality punches into the face of "some stupid young Rupert", a Rupert being a public schoolboy who's privileged youth allowed him to play at being an officer without ever having had to do any soldiering first. As an RSM, Pat had been expected to set an example other than "bopping a Rupert" who'd barked one insane order too many at him.

So, here he was, sitting in Willie's flat, which he'd turned into something resembling a crack-den within days of moving in, looking at his mobile phone, wondering who on earth was calling him from Aberdeen. Who even had his number? Willie was in Angola on Oil and Gas business. So it couldn't be him. Wait, Willie had said he'd try and set him up with a security job in the oil industry. Most companies had an office in Aberdeen. That must be it. Bloody hell, he thought. He'd better shape up – or at least shower. Maybe his period of "leave" was coming to an end. Thank Christ. Five minutes into his shower and first shave in days, the flat phone rang again, although Pat couldn't hear it as he was singing *Love Her Madly* by *The Doors* at full voice as shower water splashed all around him.

Aberdeen

Dod was sipping his cuppy downstairs patiently listening to Grumphy's directions from Rosemount to Bridge of Don Exhibition Centre. Obviously Grumphy had no interest in Dod's Sat Nav's capabilities. Dorothy was changing in her bedroom as instructed by Kylie, who was looking at the last numbers dialled on the house cordless phone. What *business* could her mum have been dealing with on a Sunday morning? One of the numbers was obviously a mobile. The other was a 0141 number. Kylie looked around the hall as she made out she was simply replacing the phone into the charger on the hall table. But nosiness got the better of her. She pressed redial. The phone rang the mobile number. It rang then went to anonymous voice mail. Her curiosity unsatisfied, Kylie called the other number, the 0141 one. It rang out.

"Come on Kylie, help Grandma sort oot these dishes."

Kylie, startled, shouted back, "Get that big lump of Dod

to help oot for a change. He's nae on the farm noo. It's equal opportunities aroon here, tell him."

"I think he heard you, quinie," shouted Grumphy, adding, "Oh, he's up, he's telling me to shhh, now he has a dishcloth in his hand, noo he's tying it roon his neck in a noose – ouch!"

"Never mind yer Granda, Kylie, he's in a funny mood," shouted Mither, slightly breathless after kicking her husband's shin.

"That'd make a change," shouted Kylie, even though she was now in the same room as everyone. The dining room cum kitchen was the family hub and had been for three generations.

Dorothy came downstairs into the room, much better dressed than before.

"Are you gan to church, Ma?"

Dorothy's face looked like Grumphy's face when he was exasperated. Some things are in the genes.

"There's no pleasing you, you little wee diva! But, if you da like it, you'll just hae to lump it.

"Fitever! Right. Can we *finally* go?"

"Here, Dod, take the map," said Grumphy.

Dod looked at Kylie and then back to Grumphy, calculating who might do him more harm if he didn't do what they wanted. It wasn't rocket science. "Sorry, Mr B, thanks for the offer, but I'll just use the Sat Nav, if that's ok?"

"Aye, aye, son, I'll just shove this map up my arse then."

All three women stood looking at Grumphy, putting their hands on their hips in a three-generational synchronised frown.

"It was a joke!" he pleaded.

"Grandma, I though you said Grumphy was in a *funny* mood."

Dod was learning how to break the ice in this family. He dangled the keys, saying, "I'm double parked guys. Let's go. The ladies can all sit in the back," he said, trying to be jocular, which was working until Grumphy added,

"Aye, but far will *that* lot sit?" he said, pointing to the formidable female formation about to leave the flat. The formation stopped walking and was about to turn round to retort. Grumphy blinked first and picked up his map from the table and said, "let's go."

Kylie and Dod looked at each other, her silently screaming, and he smiling consolingly at her until, eventually, she smiled back.

They all piled into the car, looking like they were dressed for something, except Grumphy who, with his Don's top on, was dressed only for the fitba he was looking forward to.

"Granda," said Kylie once they were all in Dod's Audi, "Silly, question, but is there any reason you are wearing a football top right now?"

"Preparations, my dear quinie, preparation."

The Three K's

Aberdeen Exhibition and Conference Centre

"Where's Grumpy noo," asked Kylie as she held up a wedding dress against her body as her mum and Grandma cooed. "He'll hae till mak sure fitever he wears matches fitever dress I choose." She looked at the snootish lady who was hoping to sell her the wedding dress and said, "Do you hae any dresses in Aberdeen colours?"

"What?"

"Just joking. My Granda will probably wear his AFC top when he gives me away."

This time the lady didn't even manage to say "what". Her face tried to get the word out but was stuck in a po-faced shape.

"Just joking, again."

"I wish you were!" said Mither. "We'll hae to peel that damn top off his back!"

"I know!" said Kylie. "I must admit, I get a wee bitty nervous when he keeps referring to walking me doon the aisle as *walking me out the tunnel*. Everything's fitba to him."

Kylie spotted Dod walking around the fair with his hands behind his back, smiling at everyone, and generally looking like he was a vaguely interested spectator rather than a central participant.

"Well? Have you seen anything on your travels?" she asked him.

Dod[looked taken aback. His mind snapped into action. What was it I was meant to see, he thought to himself. While his mind was mid-snap, Kylie interrupted.

"Cars? Kilts? Cake?"

"Ah, yes, the three Ks."

"Fit?"

"Just joking."

"You've been in Grumpy's company too long. You used to be *funny*. Talking of laugh-a-minute, far is he?"

"Umm …"

"Sticking up for him already? You're nae even under contract yet."

"Okay, I'll give you a clue. He's at one of the Ks."

Mither grasped the clue first.

"Cakes."

Dod went to walk ahead of them as all three of the ladies started to move towards Cakes, when Kylie shouted after him.

"Don't get any daft ideas about running off to warn him."

Grumphy stuck out from the crowd, being the only person in the hall with a Dons top on. There he was, dutifully trying out every sample of wedding cake going. From the pissed-off look of the cake wifies at the cake stalls Grumphy must have eaten his way through the equivalent of two tiers of wedding cake.

Mither groaned.

"George, your stomach!"

Grumphy looked round at them, piece of cake in hand, crumbs all over his Dons top and said, "Yes, it *is* mine. What's your point?"

Mither rolled her eyes. "Well, don't come crying to me later. You know how cake affects you."

"Aye, it makes me happy."

Dorothy said, "Dad, just be careful."

"Why? Are these the hash-filled cakes you once told you ate at that party in Kinneff?"

"That was *mushrooms*. And it was *Laurencekirk*. And it was *30 years ago!*"

"Mushrooms? At least you kept it vegetarian."

Dorothy looked at Mither as if to say, over to you. But Kylie stepped in to the breach.

"Granda, if you shite yourself here, you're on your own, right?"

Grumphy put the remains of the bit of cake he'd held in his hand for the duration of the row back on the cake platter on the cake stall. The cake wifie just looked at him. Grumphy looked at her and said,

"Aye, nae bad, quine. A bitty mair rum and you'd hae something there."

Dod tried to break the ice again as they walked off.

"Anyone want a hot dog?"

"Why?" asked Grumphy as they strolled along. "Have you won the lotto? Ken this? I could work for a week and still not afford that shite here. And talk about bad for your stomach? They'll kill you, these things. Pure poison."

"I'm paying."

"I'll hae een."

The ladies had given up on telling Grumphy what was good for him. Dod went off to get himself and Grumphy a hot dog.

"Granda," said Kylie, "Here, look at these kilts."

"Aye, quine, they're affa bonnie. Fit tartan's that, loon?"

The kilt mannie at the kilt stall took Grumphy's address of "loon" in good humour.

"That's the Stewart Tartan, sir."

19

"Nice. Do you have the Aberdeen Football Club tartan?"

"Err, no, I don't think so, sir. I'm not at all sure that they have a tartan, do they?"

"Getting sniffy, are we?"

"Not at all, sir. I really didn't know they had one for a football club. And I'm not sure the heritage would match that of the Stewart Tartan."

"Is that right, loon? Tell me this, then. Where were the Stewarts when the Dons were beating Bayern Munich 3-2 at Pittodrie?"

"What?"

"Nor did I see any Stewarts in Gothenburg in '83."

"Sir, I ..."

"Heritage, that's what you said wasn't it? Well, that's heritage, loon."

During the conversation Grumphy was wrapping the Stewart Tartan kilt around him, just to see how it looked. He pulled it tight against himself, then looked at Mither with a slightly panicky look on his face.

Mither whispered to Dod, "That's his cake face."

Grumphy looked around and saw the toilet sign. He moved as quickly as a 70 year old wrapped in Stewart Tartan could in the direction of the toilet with the kilt mannie shouting after him, "Sir, sir?!"

"Da worry, he'll be back," said Kylie to the kilt mannie. Then she turned to Dod, who'd just returned with two hot-dogs and said, "Fae noo on, you two are banned from cake duty, ok?"

Dod nodded, and looked apologetically at the kilt mannie, who could only imagine in horror what his kilt sample was about to be used for. Dod hesitated, then offered him the now superfluous hot-dog.

Pittodrie

Grumphy and Dod settled in their seats in The Merkland Stand at Pittodrie Stadium. The Summerhill Mob were in position too. A Dons home game was a chance to catch up on family gossip, world events and Pittodrie Pies. Dod wasn't much of a fitba fan but it was either this or lots of wifie chat about the wedding. What did he know about brides-maid dresses, or what they matched with? Even his choice of kilt was on hold until Kylie decided what wedding dress she'd chose. Besides. It'd give him a chance to have a bonding blether with Grumphy.

Dod waved to the Summerhill Mob. They had a decent turnout today. Eight of them were season holders and they sat just a few rows behind Grumphy and co, who had three season tickets. But, with Mither and Kylie otherwise engaged in wedding discussions post-Wedding Fair, it was just Dod and Grumphy and an empty seat this time. Dorothy hated football. "The fitba gene skipped a generation" Grumphy used to say, often adding, "A tragic condition".

Dod and Grumphy has parked near the Pittodrie Bar after dropping the quines back home and now they were "two pints to the good" as Grumphy put it.

The game started and Grumphy adopted his fitba analysis stance; sitting up straight with his cap keeping the sun out his eyes and with both arms folded, watching the game with an intensity surpassed only by Derek McInnes, the Don's manager.

"So, how do you think we'll do today?" asked Dod.

21

Grumphy never took his eyes off the action as he replied, "Are you trying ti mak conversation?"

Dod was a bit taken aback, but replied that he was.

"Well, dinna."

That was that then. Dod tried to get into the game but his mind strayed, only brought back to it when the crowd reacted to some drama on the pitch. But he was behind the pace and when he'd worked out what had happened on the park to cause the crowd to boo, he booed too, but a few seconds after it mattered. The same when he cheered, or groaned.

"You're lacking match fitness, son," said Grumphy without barely moving his lips.

It wasn't just Dod's lack of interest in football that caused his mind to stray. There were some big issues relating to the wedding that would need dealing with. Not the nitty gritty details. That's what quines were for, thought Dod, meaning they were good at it. No, what was on his mind was his fiancée's father. Kylie only once had mentioned that she wished she'd known her dad. She was a go-getter, and a getter-on with things. She didn't stop and think about life's big issues very often. But, when they'd gotten engaged at Stonehaven harbour one sunny summer night, Kylie had, after accepting Dod's proposal, asked almost involuntarily, "But fa will give me awa?"

Dod had said they could find out about her father quite easily these days. But Kylie didn't want to upset her mum who apparently didn't ever want to talk about him. Her mum had got herself together as a single parent in the eighties and in the nineties she'd made a reasonable living as an illustrator, greetings cards, books and such like. She'd never really tried Art at school but she had been determined to do something different after Kylie had been born and found that she was very good at it. It fed both her and Kylie and, from time to time, Grumphy and Mither too. What did she need a man for?

But Dod knew that deep down this was something Kylie had to do one day. So why not before the wedding? That's why he'd spoken to Kylie's mum, Dorothy on the QT about it just after the engagement. Dorothy had reacted furiously to Dod "interfering in family affairs" but after a few weeks she'd calmed down, calling him to apologise and to say that he was family too now. But that she needed time to think about getting in touch with Kylie's father. She'd had no contact since she'd left for Tarbert 25 years before. She wouldn't know where to start.

Dod wanted to sound Grumphy out about Kylie's father. He knew nothing about this guy and no one ever talked about it. And who was Dod to rattle the bones in someone else's cupboard? However, he loved his quine and he knew her well. He knew she thought about it more than she let on.

The Don's game seemed quiet enough. Now might be a good time to seek the head of the family's advice.

"Mr B ..."

Grumphy didn't answer. His armed stayed folded, and the cap on his head didn't flinch as he stared at the pitch."

"Mr B ..." said Dod a little louder this time.

"Dod," said Grumphy without moving a muscle.

"Yes?"

"Just coz you got a free seat for the game on account of Mither no coming the day doesny mean you can yap awa throughoot the game like she does."

"But Mr B ..."

"Haud on noo. Are you awa to say it's important?"

"Aye."

23

"Okay, then."

Dod leant over to speak and got as far as opening his mouth before Grumphy raised one hand, saying,

"Wait till hauf time, min."

Attention!

Glasgow

"Willie!" Good to hear you, man. Yes, everything's fine, pal. The flat?" Pat looked around the flat and at the couple of holes in the wall that he'd made with his fists when frustration and drink had combined to get the better of him, and at the two-week's worth of dishes piled precariously in the sink and the obstacle course of beer cans and stains on the carpet. ""Aye, aye, it's ... fine. Perfect in fact. The washing machine? Aye, it works, mate." That was a guess from Pat who'd not washed a thing since he'd arrived. "Everything's tip top, Willie. So, when is it your back? Tomorrow! I thought you said two weeks? ... Was it really, two weeks ago, huh. Time flies, mate ... You're in London just now ... right, right ... I've nowhere sorted just yet but I'm sure I will. No problem. See you then."

Pat looked around the room again and the mission formed instantly in his mind. Four hours later, the place was spotless, like he'd never been there. An internet plasterer was coming that afternoon to sort out the walls. Pat had just about enough cash to cover the agreed cost. He took the precaution of putting all the empty beer cans in a neighbours bin. What did he care? He was out on his ear tomorrow anyway.

Then he remembered what he should have asked Willie. So he called him back.

"Willie, what about this job thing you've got me fixed

up with … the one that called me this morning, or was it afternoon? I cannae mind, but I'm sure it was today, ha ha. What d'ya mean, 'what job?'? An Aberdeen number called me this morning. And you're the only person I've given this number to. Oh, and someone called Debbie, apparently. Sit down? What do I want to sit down for? Actually, I *am* sitting down already. Do you want me to stand up and then sit down again, for effect? No no no. You've obviously got something to say, don't wait until tomorrow to tell me. I'm sitting down especially, remember? I'm sitting down like I've never sat down before! What d'ya mean you'll tell me when we meet! Willie? Willie?"

Pat called Willie back but no reply. "Well that does it," said Pat out loud. "I'm standing the f*** up."

What was going on? Willie obviously chickened out of telling him something important. He sat back down. He got his phone out again. He looked at the number. "Aberdeen," he muttered quietly, staring at the phone screen again. Now, apart from some kind of job search related thing, the only Aberdeen connections were from 25 years ago. Pat's subconscious was placing pieces of a long broken jig-saw together. Pat's conscious mind was lagging behind his subconscious, partly due to a haze built up over four weeks of alcohol intake, and partly because some events from 25 years ago had been too traumatic to think about since they occurred. Pat's heart was stirring. Dare he hope that something beautiful might be happening? And what did Willie know that he didn't?

The mobile he was staring at beeped. It was a text from Willie.

"Get your stuff packed. We're going to Aberdeen in the morning. Pick you up at 9am."

Oh well. Clearly there'd be no resolution of this mystery until Willie showed up in the morning. He left the key under the mat as agreed with the plasterer, and, as agreed with himself, went out and got drunk.

Take Me Home Country Roads

"Willie?"

"Oh, so you're awake?"

Willie had picked up Pat at 9am as agreed. They were on the road to Aberdeen. No amount of polite chit chat was going to keep Pat from sleeping off his hangover and he'd lapsed into snoring mode by Cumbernauld.

"Where are we?"

"Scummers."

"Scummers? Already?" Yer, making good time, Willie."

Scummers was what Pat and Willie called Dundee. Some less than respectful Aberdeen fans called Dundee "Scumdee", alluding to the rivalry between the North East's two cities. Pat and Willie had abbreviated Scumdee to Scummers for no reason they could remember.

"Are we stopping at Bervie?"

"What for?"

"Pop into The Sally (The Salutation Hotel) for a few."

"Aye, that's great. You get steaming and I'll sit and watch. Is that your plan? Coz, it's no mine."

The hum of the car motoring along was uninterrupted as Pat reconciled himself to the fact that this might be the first sober day in four weeks.

"Are you no going to ask why we're going to Aberdeen?"

"Work?"

"Maybe. But that's not all."

"Well, seeing as I've no family, friends or any other earthly reason to go back to Donsville, it's no a social visit."

"Hold on. What did you just say?"

"What about? Social visit?"

"No, before that."

"No friends?"

"Before that."

"No family?"

Once again the hum of the drive took over as Willie went silent. Pat, who'd been slouched against the passenger window looked over at Willie, and then sat up properly.

"I said, 'no family', and you shut up?"

Willie sighed. "You know what? Maybe we could pop into The Sally on the way."

"Willie, you always were a truly brilliant procrastinator. And right now, I'm awe once again. Don't get me wrong. Part of me is losing flipping patience – but part of me is in awe."

"Somethings just aren't easy to say."

"Or to hear. But f*** it, Willie, the sooner you spill the beans the sooner I can go as mental you think I'm going to go, and then we can all just get on with it."

"Alright. But don't shoot the messenger, ok?"

"Willie, we know each other's darkest secrets, don't we? I think all the shooting was done a long time ago, buddy. Pull over here and we'll get a coffee. I've got a feeling I'll need it."

Willie pulled into Stracathro services. Pat took a seat and Willie brought over two coffees.

"Right, Willie. Why are going to Aberdeen? I mean, I could just ring this number here, the one that called me? I only called it back once and got no reply. But, hey, I could call again?"

"She was never meant to phone that number before she talked to me first."

"Who's 'she'?"

29

"Who do you think?"

"I've not the faintest idea, mate!"

"Really? You can't put 'Aberdeen' and 'she' into an idea?"

Pat felt the jigsaw pieces fall a little more together, uncomfortably.

"Willie, I know you want me to say it for you."

"Good."

"And God knows I'll wait decades for you to tell me." Pat took a breath and said, "Dorothy?"

Willie looked out the window, and then back at his cup, and said, "Aye."

Pat looked out the window now, but couldn't see anything to distract himself from the quiet grenade Willie had thrown him.

"So, we're going to see Dorothy?" said Pat quietly.

"Aye."

"Jeezo, Willie, I thought I'd had all the shocks I'd ever need at my age. Dorothy, a fine quine. I really messed that one up."

"No you didn't. You were just young. You weren't for settling."

"But I was, Willie, I was. I just didn't know it."

"Aye, you look like you really settled down, mate. Look at you. 25 years of roaming the planet, and the last four weeks in Pintsville. You're the original wild rover."

"No, Willie. It's not like that."

"Anyway, you'd better get ready for a bit of shock."

"You mean that wasn't it?"

Willie realised that he'd opened another can of worms without meaning to. He sighed, and sat back in his seat, muttering, "shit."

Pat stared at Willie, looking for clues. Willie's reticence was driving him crazy, but part of him didn't want to know.

"Is Dorothy married?"

Willie, looked at Pat, "no."

"Dead?"

"No, of course not. How could we going to meet her if she was dead."

"Tell me, Willie, why do you know something about Dorothy that I don't?"

Willie, leant over, putting his elbows on the table.

"Look. You disappeared from Bervie. No one knew where you went. Sure, I helped you, I took care of a few things for you when you buggered off. We were best mates and that's what we do, right? Then like a year after you'd left, I bump into Dorothy in the Deen, on Union Street. We got talking about you and she got really upset. In fact, she said, she wished she'd never let you go. You'd told me never to tell anyone where you went. So I didn't tell her. She didn't want you back, but just wanted to know you were ok. And she told me that if you ever came back, would I let her know. So, I took her number."

"And you never told me."

"How would I have done that, then? Telepathy? See, Pat, it's all very well disappearing, all heartbroken and dramatic and that. But I didn't know where you were."

"Gutersloh."

"Not all the time. You never replied to the letter I wrote to you there, 25 years ago, mate! In fact, until you got in touch last month, I didn't know if you were alive or dead, although I figured I'd hear about your death if it happened because, doubtless, there'd have been some shite to pick up somewhere."

"Well, she's the one who dumped me, by the way, not the other way around. I'm not going to feel guilty about having had a life. She had her chance."

"Maybe it was a bit more complicated than that, Pat."

"Nothing's complicated, Willie, everything's simple. I wanted to marry her and everything. Settle down. Have kids, the whole thing. But she kicked me in the teeth."

"To be fair, only after you'd kicked her in the teeth a hundred times. Cancelling dates, behaving like you were single when you were dating her."

"Okay, I was dating her. But I WAS single."

"Pat, you're a scream. See, when you date a girl, you're not actually single."

"I don't mean I cheated on her. You know I never did."

"I know."

"But I mean I still had things to do, songs to write, bands to run."

"You were a salesman!"

"Aye, but only till I'd saved up some dosh, do to do my real stuff, music and that."

"That's all dandy. But here you are, 25 years later. And she wants to see you. Don't tell her you've got songs to write, for flip's sake."

"Why?"

"Because that's the last thing she'll want to hear!"

"No, I mean, why does she want to see me?"

"Ah."

"What do you mean, 'ah'? Wait, let me guess, is this where the next shock comes in?"

Willie looked like he was thinking about saying something. Then he stopped himself, and simply said, "Aye".

Pat looked at him intently, then made a rolling gesture with his hands, as if to say, c'mon then."

"Pat, have you ever heard that song, *We're Not Alone*?" Willie, sang it quietly.

32

"The song you're thinking of is called, I think, *We're All Alone*."

"Is it?"

"Aye".

"Oh well, scrub that."

"Willie, see if you were ever to brief troops on a mission, there'd be death all around.

"Look, I think it would be better if Dorothy told you herself."

"Aye, I think it might. And if not better, then at least quicker, you muppet."

Pittodrie – The 2nd Half.

The half-time whistle blew and the crowd cheered as the Dons were a goal up. Dod started cheering too, but just after the crowd had stopped. Dod stopped suddenly, with a few bemused regulars wondering what Dod was all about. Grumphy caught the eye of one those fans just in front of him and Dod and shook his head, saying to the fan, "It's his first game." The bemused fan, nodded sympathetically, realising that Grumphy was sitting beside someone who could not contribute to his understanding of the first half's events. Dod went to say something when Grumphy interrupted him before he'd even started.

"You still here?

"Dod looked around, adding, sarcastically, "apparently."

"Right, so, in other words, what your saying is I'll hae till ging a the way up these stairs to get my ain Pittodrie Pie? And me a pensioner."

"You mean there isn't a guy who brings them round?"

Dod could see a few of the heads wrapped up in red and white AFC woolly hats in front of them shaking as they'd obviously overheard his query.

"Aye," said Grumphy, "jist after the masseuse, but jist before the cabaret." The heads in hats in front shook a little, along with the attached shoulders in AFC shirts. "Tell, me Dod, is this what it's like at the rugby?"

"Look, Mr B, I was wondering …"

"Where the pie stall is? I've told ye, It's at the top of the stairs. Noo, ging up there and get oor pies afore they're sold oot, or ging oot o date. Then, if there's time, you can spik awa aboot fitever ye like."

Dod found himself in the queue. The smell of the pies was alluring, no doubt. He waited what seemed ages in the queue but before long he was back in the seats with two pies. Only problem was Grumphy wasn't there. Dod was then distracted by jeers from the crowd directed at the referee who, it seemed, had some paternity issues. "He's not the only one," thought Dod, as he considered the whole reason for wanting to speak to Grumpy. Talking of Grumphy ...

"You jist sit there, Dod, dinna get up. I'll jist stand here in the aisle a day."

"Sorry Mr B, can you not squeeze passed?" said Dod, getting up.

"I've jist done enough squeezin' fir one day," said Grumphy as he bumped his way back to his seat.

"Have I missed onyhin?"

One of the fans in the row in front turned his neck around and Grumphy saw eyes between the lower edge of a Dons hat and the upper edges of a Dons scarf. "The referee's a bastard!"

"I kent that already. So, I didna miss onyhing. Ah, thanks Dod." Grumphy took both pies from Dod. "Did ye no get een for yersel?"

Dod's mouth fell open.

"Ach, here, shove this in your pie hole afore ye swallow a seagull. I was kidding."

"Mr B?"

"Aw, fit noo?"

"About that chat?"

"It's rude to spik wi yer moo foo."

"But I'm not eating anything yet."

"Aye, well, start for flip's sake, and dinna stop until the final whistle."

Walking the Mat.

Grumphy could walk a fair pace for his age thought Dod as they walked up Union street. The car was parked up safely and after another couple of what Grumphy had described as "quick ones" in the Pittodrie Bar there was no way Dod would drive. Grumphy liked the fresh air and relative quiet after the noise and stuffiness of the pub. They were now, as Grumphy would have put it, four pints to the good. This gave Dod a bit of Dutch courage, as did the fact that Grumphy was quite jolly as the Dons had won.

"It's not a race, Mr B," he said laughing.

"Just working up a thirst, loon. But, if you're struggling, just sit here and I'll see if I can flag doon the St John's Ambulance folk tae tak you hame." Grumphy marched on.

"A thirst? We've just had a drink."

"That was King Street. This is Union Street. It's a different jurisdiction here, loon. We hae til hae a pint in each street. Besides, think of all the wifie chat going on back at the ranch. Do you really want to get back for that?"

"Well, why did we not just stay in the Pittodrie Bar?"

"Got to at least be seen to be making an effort to get hame."

"I don't get it."

"Dod, consider this a free lesson on how to stay married and still hae some freedom. Think, min. Any minute now, one of the quines will look at her watch and figure out the game's been over for 45 minutes. At that point, our mobile phones will ring. Our whereabouts will be inquired about.

36

Now, this way, we can, hand on heart, say that we are on Union Street. And that we're haein' a pint. The quines will surmise that we are, in theory, only few minties awa. In the world of fly-pinting, 'minties awa' can legitimately be anything from twa minties to 180 minties, although, I admit, that's pushing it a wee bitty."

Dod was rolling his eyes mentally before he said, "Mr B, there's a whole lot more to learn that I thought."

"Scoff if you want, loon," said Grumphy, seeing through Dod's sarcasm immediately. "But, believe, me, five minutes into yer marriage you'll be begging for such lessons."

"Ha ha. Well, I suppose my old man will have a few tips."

"Sure, what would he know? He's only fae Echt. This is big city stuff, loon."

Soon Grumphy and Dod were in *The Stag*. Grumphy, looked up at one of the big screens. "Mair fitba? Oh min, we've done oor duty the day. We dinna hae to watch this pish."

"It's Man United."

"So fit? Da tell me, you dinna watch *fitba*, but you do watch ...," Grumphy put on false heirs and spat out the word, *Football?"

"What's the difference?"

"*Fitba* is fit mannies watch. *Football* is for gloryhunters."

"What do you mean?"

"Put it this way. Fit part of Manchester are you fae?"

"Eh?"

"Is Echt near Mossside? Or Old Trafford?"

"Mr B, I ..."

"Ken fit I mean? We follow The Dons because that's oor toon. Fa gives a shite aboot Man United, or Chelsea, or, God help us, Barcel-flipping-ona? You follow your ain team, nae the een wi the biggest crowds, or the richest players fa canna stand to get kicked a wee bitty wi oot fawn to the deck like they've been hit by a sniper."

Dod sipped his pint. There wasn't much point in pretending he had a clue what Grumphy was on about. But he felt obliged to take a shot at it.

"So, what you're saying is that I should support Echt?"

Grumphy had his pint too close to his lips to slow down its journey. Besides, what could he say? He sipped his lager, then eventually replied.

"Dod, technically, you're right. But let's nae be extreme about it."

"But that's my town."

"Echt's no a toon, loon. It's a village. A very nice village. But you should support the Dons."

Dod, feeling slightly brave due to having three pints more than his normal limit of one, said, "But wouldn't that make me a glory hunter?"

Grumphy looked stumped. But his face lit up like a thought had just occurred.

"No. Because Echt is in Aberdeenshire."

"But Aberdeenshire's not a town."

Bloody hell, thought, Grumphy. The loon might no be a drinker, but he can still land a punch from the ropes. He smiled at Dod who was just trying to look sober. "Same again, loon?"

"Shouldn't we be getting back?"

"We're at base camp here, within striking distance of the summit. So, there's nae rush. Besides, has your phone rung yet?"

"No?"

"Exactly. We come when called. Not before. Same again?"

After being told it was his round, Dod found his way back

to the table gingerly with two pints. He sat down beside Grumphy. He was sober enough to realise he had to talk to Grumphy about Kylie's father now or never. Grumphy was sufficiently relaxed now to listen.

"Mr B?"

"Gan then. Fit are ye wanting to nip my ears aboot?"

"I'm just trying to work out if it's worthwhile contacting Kylie's dad, about the wedding I mean."

Grumphy's face didn't flinch. Dod had no way of knowing if this direct approach was working or not. There was silence. Then Grumphy said,

"She's nae got a 'Dad'. She has, regrettably, a 'faither'. But that's nae the same thing at a. So, unless there's a law that says we hae tae, I da think we will be hain' onyhin' tae dae wi her 'faither', so-called."

That went much better than I thought it might, thought Dod to himself. He went to speak but Grumphy interrupted."

"Has she said anything about him, like? She must have, or you'd nae hae been thinking aboot it."

"Not really, but I know she thinks about it more than she says. I mean, who wouldn't?"

Grumphy sipped his pint. Then he turned to Dod.

"I know you care about my granddaughter. She's mair like a daughter to me. She's done very well for herself. She's got her degree. She's going to be a teacher. She's never had the all the complications of dealing with dodgy relations. But, I've always said to myself that if she wanted to find oot about Pat, then I wouldna stand in her way."

"That's … that's noble of you, Mr B."

"Aye, but fitever happens, I'll be geein' her awa."

"Quite right, Mr B. You said, 'Pat'. I suppose that's her dad's name?"

"No. It's her faither's name."

"Father, yes. Father. What do you know about him?"

"Mair than I'll ever want to ken."

"Was he a bad guy?"

"Some would say no. But, he broke my daughter's heart. So, fit would you expect me to say. I guessing Kylie doesna ken your spicking to me about this."

"No. But I have talked to someone else about it."

"Fa?"

"Her mum."

"Aye? And how'd that go? Well?" Grumphy laughed."

"Well. Eventually."

"Fan was this?"

"A couple of weeks ago. She's of the same opinion as you."

"Well, it seems that everyone thinks the same. So, I suppose we'd better spick to the een person fa should be telt."

"What about Mrs B?"

"Mither will ging alang wi' fitever I suggest."

Dod, well on now from an uncommon amount of pints, said, "Ha ha. No, but really …"

Grumphy laughed into his pint, adding, "Aye, Mither will ging alang wi fitever I suggest, once she's telt me fit to suggest."

Almost in unison, both their phones rang. Without picking up his phone, Grumphy said, "Time to climb the North Face of Rosemount."

40

Just South of Hanoi

Willie came back to the car. He'd been on his mobile phone. Pat had been sleeping and was only now waking up. He looked around. They were in a car park. It was a Sainsburys. But he'd no idea where. It was a built up area, so, he guessed, unless Bervie had grown beyond recognition they must be in Aberdeen. He got out the car. Willie was saying his goodbyes on the phone. The cold air hit Pat's face. The air was chiller than Glasgow. That was for sure.

"Where are we, Wilie?"

"Vietnam. Where d'ya think we are?"

Pat looked around, he saw a large Asda store over the way and semi recognised the hill with houses on it. He also saw what looked like a practise ski slope.

"'Nam, huh. It's gone downhill, Willie?"

"Aye, we're in downtown Hanoi, just south of Garthdee."

"Garthdee?" Pat smiled as 25 year-old memories thawed in his mind. "Man, we had some fun here. Do you mind we used to scoosh the Asda guys in the car park with our windae washers tampered with so they fired at whoever we drove passed?"

"Aye, "laughed Willie, "Didn't we christen them after TV guys they looked like?"

"Ha ha, aye. Alan Wicker and Sandy Gall!"

"Aye, but they could fair run when they were angry."

"Aye, they didn't like being scooshed."

"Who did!?"

"Mind they took to throwing clumps of earth and stones at us whenever they saw the car?"

"Aye, it was like 'Nam, right enough."

"Do you mind we used to drive up and down Union Street, scooshing the bus queues?"

"Aye, and mind we had to break a red light when one bus queue worked out what was going on and then came after us with brick?"

"That's Torry for you."

"Hee hee."

"Aye, but as always, you took it too far."

"Eh?"

"You ended up buying water pistols for us all."

"Ha ha, aye, and then we did a hit on Alan Wicker and Sandy Gall, a drive by water pistoling."

"Jeez, aye. Mind they ended up ramming Asda trollies at the motor, water dripping off their faces"

"Aye, well. We were young."

"In our 20s, Pat!"

"Aye, like I said, young."

They let their laughter die down.

"How you feeling, Pat?"

"Hangover's gone, just in time too, it must be time for a pint."

Willie smiled and started walking towards the Sainsbury entrance. Pat could see there was a café next to the entrance. He shouted after Willie, as he started to follow him.

"I guess the pint will wait a bit longer then?"

"Aye," shouted back Willie, walking on.

Pat caught him up just as they walked into Sainsbury.

"Coffee, Willie? I'll get these, mate."

Willie caught him by the arm and said,

"You go on in to the café, I'll catch you up. Don't get me anything."

Pat looked at him. What was going on? Willie gave him a hug and said, "Good luck mate." Willie then walked out, leaving Pat stranded. Pat shouted after him, "What the hell, Willie, am I in a David Lynch film or something?" Willie didn't hear him or if he did he just kept walking. Pat, exasperated, went to the till to buy coffee.

In the army, Pat had developed what many soldiers in intelligence develop – a uniquely strong sixth sense. Before the mannie at the till could ask Pat what he would like, Pat span around and looked over at the window. There were tables there. At one of them sat a handsome middle-aged lady, quite prim and proper looking, well dressed. She must have felt Pat's stare as she looked up from the phone she'd just been looking at. Pat's legs went to jelly.

"What would you like sir?" asked the café mannie
"A double brandy."

Empty Chair

"Where have you two been?" asked Mither as Dod and Grumphy strolled in.

"We were jist hanging back a bitty, jist to keep oot yer way until you had supper sorted oot?"

Mither looked at Grumphy. Then at Dod. Then she said, to neither of them in particular, "how many has he had?" Dod and Grumphy answered at the same time but with different numbers, Dod saying "four" and Grumphy saying "jist a couple".

Kylie came in from the hallway. "Aye, a couple of gallons! Dod, I hope you're not thinking of getting a season ticket. Your liver will be done by Christmas." Dod then clumsily mumbled something about scaling the North Face and about Pinting Minties until Grumphy interrupted saying, "What he means is it'll no happen again." He looked around and saw the table set for four.

"Fa's no eating wi us?"

"Dorothy," said Mither.

"How come?"

"She's got a trap!" said Kylie, excitedly.

"Well, no, she hasn't got a trap," said Mither. "She's just seeing an old friend."

"Aye? Fa's that, then?" asked Grumphy.

"She'll tell you herself, George. Da be so nosey."

Dod sat down and was beginning to so sober up. Rapidly.

44

The Slippery Slopes
of Garthdee

She just looks the same, thought Pat. Older, but the same. Pat's mind scattered into pieces. There seemed to be fragments of times gone by fluttering around everywhere. A voice intruded into this mental landscape.

"Sorry, sir, we're not licensed. Not in the café anyway. Can I get you a coffee or tea?"

Pat, looked back round at the café mannie. "Tea, son, please. Thanks." He looked back at the table by the window with the woman who looked the same but different. He broke into a big smile. He couldn't help it. The woman smiled back. Was he dreaming?

"That'll be £1.80 please, sir."

No, it wasn't a dream. He paid for his tea, looked around and wondered if he really should go over and join the lady by the window. Actually, he knew he should but, he wondered if he could. His courage was being slow to appear. The lady, however, turned in her chair and looked at him with a slightly admonishing look. She always did have enough courage for the both of them. Then she smiled. It was always less dangerous approaching a woman if she was smiling. Especially if you hadn't seen her for a quarter of a century. Pat smiled back. And walked over with his tea, thinking to himself, "Ah, Willie, what have you done."

"Dorothy," said Pat.

Dorothy, smiled again. "Yes, Pat. At least I haven't aged so much you didn't recognised me."

"At least I was sober enough to," said Pat laughing, but realising instantly he'd probably made better jokes. Thankfully, Dorothy breezed over the silly comment with,

"Sit down, Pat." Pat went to sit down but Dorothy interrupted, "I meant after you've given me a hug!"

Pat laughed nervously and hugged her. It was a real hug. She smelled so nice and felt so comfortable. He let go even though he didn't want to. And sat down.

The hug seemed to unbalance Dorothy, but she recovered to sit down too.

"Well, this is a surprise," laughed Pat. "Well, a surprise to me at least."

"You mean Willie didn't tell you?"

"What do you think?" said Pat. "When has Willie ever gotten to the point?"

"Ha ha. God, yes. Thank goodness it's not just me! He's impossible to get any info out of! I wasn't sure if you were coming today or not?"

"I didn't know myself where I was even coming to!"

"Didn't you ask Willie?"

"Yes!"

They both laughed.

"What did he tell you, Pat?"

"Very little!"

"He must have told you something? He told me four weeks ago that you were coming to Aberdeen."

"That was nice of him. He told me yesterday I was coming to Aberdeen."

They laughed again.

"Still," said, Dorothy, "here you are."

Pat looked at her. "Yes, here I am."

They looked at each other for a minute.

"Have you been ill, Pat? You look drawn."

"I've had a rough few weeks. But I'm feeling better today."

"What was it? Flu? A virus? A bevy?"

Pat looked at her smiling. "You know, I didn't have a drink for nearly 20 years after we ... lost touch."

"Okay, but that leaves another 5 years unaccounted for," replied Dorothy, light-heartedly.

"If, only I could remember them."

They both laughed out loud. Pat continued.

"I'm kidding. Even the last 5 years I hardly touched the stuff. But when I did, it would be for a few days at a time. Seemed best to do it properly, or not at all."

"A real pro."

"Aye. What about you?"

"What? You mean my drinking habits?"

Pat was about to say "no" but instead changed direction and said, "Aye, how's your drinking?"

"Ha ha. Same as it always was. Moderate to fair."

They both laughed again.

After the ice-breaking banter, a silence came over them as they sipped their drinks, both desperate to ask each other about a million things. But as silences go, it was a comfortable one. Not awkward. In fact, if it wasn't for the fact they'd lived their lives in different continents for 25 years, it seemed like they'd never been apart.

Pat held back a bit. He was enjoyed this feeling and didn't want it to end right way. Obviously the meeting wasn't really about their drinking habits or about Willie. But, now that Pat had the chance to find out what it was about, he found that he wasn't sure if he wanted to.

Dorothy knew she was doing the right thing. She was not looking forward to telling Pat that he had a daughter he'd

47

never known about. She felt terrible guilt about not telling him. Suddenly she was mentally back on the bus 25 years ago with the dilemma of whether to tell Pat or not that she was pregnant. Now, quarter of a century later, that baggage was still unpacked.

Pat wasn't stupid. It was just that he'd had less than a day to sober up, and then work out that he was in Aberdeen, far less have time to consider all the possibilities as to why he was meeting Dorothy.

But, they both knew it was time to talk.

"Pat. I've a few things to tell you. I've got a lot of things to ask you, too. And just so you know, that regardless of what I've got to say, this isn't a 'getting back together' scenario."

Pat was taken aback. How could Dorothy even think he'd consider getting back together? Sure, life could be better. But he also knew it could be worse. No, he was happy the way things were. And if he wasn't really, then he would be once he got himself together. Last thing he needed was any new commitments.

"Well, to be honest, that suits me just fine. I'm too old to consider romance."

"I'm the same age as you!" She laughed

"Well, then I must be younger than I thought." He smiled.

"Still the charmer."

Pat's curiosity was returning.

"So, if you're not proposing marriage, what is it you want to tell me?"

"Well, I'm glad you're sitting down."

"What is it with you and Willie? Both of you are very keen on me sitting down."

"Pat, I know I should have told you this way before now. But please, please, try and understand why I didn't. I was desperate for you to be happy forever. I truly loved you.

But I wasn't selfish enough to tie you down before you were ready. I wanted you to do everything your heart was set on. I wanted you to chase your dreams. I wanted your happiness so much and I didn't think I could give you that."

Pat's heart was beating. Just hearing Dorothy tell him how she'd once felt opened a door inside him and a torrent of emotions that had been kept at bay for years suddenly flooded through. This was shock enough, but he knew she was saying all this for a reason. He said nothing.

"Pat, when we're young, we think we know what's best for everyone, and for ourselves. But we just don't." Her eyes were a bit watery, thought Pat. She felt Pat's hand clasp hers on the table. Pat hadn't even been aware of doing so. Then her other hand clasped Pat's. "I am scared to tell you what I need to tell you because I think you'll hate me, and I think you might be right."

"Dorothy, whatever has happened I will never hate you, ever. I was angry for a long time. But I came to see that there's more to everything. It's like Willie says, life is complex.

"You got that insight from Willie?" She laughed nervously. A joke to stall the inevitable.

"Ha ha, yeah, a rare moment of lucidity on his part." He held her hand a bit tighter. "Whatever it is, don't forget that I know that you're a beautiful person. And if you've made any kind of mistake, which I doubt, then I'd still think that."

Dorothy was feeling the same trembling inside that Pat was. She could feel him shaking slightly in her hand. She knew deep down he was a good person too and after 25 years of not telling him, it was time now.

"Pat, I have a daughter, a beautiful daughter."

Pat looked at her and saw her in pain. "It's okay. It's okay. I'm glad you have a daughter. Is she okay?"

"Yes, she is, she's a little wee wonder."

"And you thought I'd be upset? Jesus, don't put yourself through all that for no reason. How old is she?"

Dorothy knew it was now or never. "She's 24."

"All grown up, eh?"

Dorothy looked at him, "Yeah, all grown up, Pat, all grown up." She wiped a tear from eye.

"24, eh. What's she do?"

"She's starting a primary school teacher job in August. Look, Pat, do the maths."

Pat had been doing just that ever since Dorothy had said '24'.

"Pat, my daughter is your daughter."

Although he'd begun to see this coming a few moments before it still hit him like a rock. He was stunned. His life story it seemed had just been rewritten in a second. But he continued to hold her hand. She was the author of a whole chapter of his life that he knew nothing of. He needed to know his whole story. And he now needed to know Dorothy's whole story. And her daughter's. His daughter's.

"I'm trying hard to imagine why you didn't tell me?"

"Because …"

"I know what you said. I'm trying to put myself in your shoes. I know I must have given the impression that I wasn't ready for settling down. But didn't your family tell you that I'd come round to your house? That I'd made up my mind to settle down with you?"

Dorothy took one of her hands off his. "But Pat, it wasn't as if that was the only time you'd said all that."

"But I meant it that time."

"You said you meant it the time before when you said it. And the time before that."

50

In Pat's mind he'd only ever given his "settling down" speech once. But Dorothy's comments started his mind re-reading decades old memories a little more carefully. She was right. All these years he'd felt hard done by because Dorothy's family was not interested in his conversion because as Grumphy had put it, Pat went to Damascus and back on a weekly basis.

"I know. I know. But I truly meant it that time. Did you know I went to Tarbert the day after you did?"

"I only found that out after you'd left."

"Didn't that show you I was serious?"

"Yes, it did."

"Why didn't you try to find me?"

"You mean after you'd told the only person who knew where you'd gone never to tell anyone?"

"Willie."

"Yes."

"He said you bumped into him on Union Street."

"Eh? I tracked him down more like. But he wouldn't tell me where you were."

"Did you tell him you were pregnant?"

"I'd had Kylie by then."

"Kylie. Nice name. I guess it's too late for my suggestions."

"Pat. You ran away!"

"You ran away first!"

"I was scared!"

"And I wasn't?"

They sat in silence until Pat asked,

"Why now?"

"Because there's something else."

"Great. Another surprise. Look, before you tell me any-more, tell me about Kylie. A teacher you say? Does she look like you or me? What colour is her hair? Is she a happy girl? What did you tell her about me? Does she ask about me?"

"Well, she has red hair, and before you ask, it's too late to do a paternity test."

Maybe it was too early to lighten the mood. But she had to try. Pat though was clearly not ready to have a laugh about it all. He sat back and sighed. None of their hands were touching.

Pat eventually, said, "My mother had red hair."

"I wish I'd met her," said Dorothy. Pat's mother had died when he was 12, which Dorothy had known. But it had been natural to wonder who the man she loved at the time had come from.

"Now, let me try and answer your questions. She is a very happy girl. She's indomitable. Don't suppose any child of ours would have had any choice in that department."

Pat smiled. He was still in shock. He was warming to the fact he had a daughter, but was still furious inside that he had never known about her until now. Still, he knew he had to ride these emotions or he'd end up doing or saying something he'd regret. He had enough regrets.

"So, does she look like you or me?"

Dorothy looked at him and said, with some pride, "Both of us. She has your eyes. She reminds me of you every day."

"Is that a good thing?" said Pat, with no more than a hint of sarcasm.

"I like to think so. You were the love of my life. And I'm very proud of my …our daughter."

Pat nodded, as if he approved of her answer, although he realised that Dorothy needed no one's approval, despite seeming to want his just now.

A daughter. My god. His daughter! It was all sinking in.

"I'm guessing she knows nothing about me."

Dorothy nodded, a little ashamed.

"Well, looks like I'm not the only one who's in for a shock.

The Trap

Kylie was concerned. Her mother, Dorothy, had not returned from her get-together with her old friend and/or trap. And the fact that her Grandma, Mither, did not appear concerned was in itself concerning because what it meant was that Mither knew something that Kylie didn't, and that was always a concern.

"Grandma? Why do I have the feeling that you know more than you are telling about my Ma's trap?"

"It's nae a trap, quine, I've told you that."

"Aye, that's all you've telt me. Tell me this – fa was Ma calling this morning?"

"Oh, how should I know? Now, here, dry these."

"Passing the buck, eh?" Kylie was smiling as she took the plates from Mither. But, she was intrigued, which meant it was only a matter of time before the truth would be uncovered. Mither knew this, but she realised her mission was to hold off Kylie's march towards the truth until Dorothy got back.

Kylie sensed Mither was not for spilling. She turned round from the sink, where she and Mither were dealing with the dishes, and looked over at the two snoring men sleeping off the concoction of pints and Sunday supper. They were vulnerable in that post-boozy afterglow. No time to compare notes, no time to look at each other for direction – not if Kylie rudely awoke them right now, anyway. Mither went through to her and Grumphy's bedroom to put new sheets on the bed.

Kylie knelt down beside Grumphy and whispered. "Granda." She shook him slightly. No response. Kylie shook Grumphy again, whispering slightly louder this time, "Granda." Grumphy's snoring didn't waver. She eyed him suspiciously. She knew he was a master. So she turned her attention to his less than masterful apprentice and knelt beside Dod. "Dod. Wake up, now," she said firmly. Dod spluttered and opened his eyes even though he couldn't possibly have been awake. Kylie clapped her hands loudly twice, one beside each of Dod's ears. Now not only his eyes were open but his head was shaking slightly and his mouth involuntarily muttered "what?"

"Were you sleeping, Dod?"

"No, honey, just resting my eyes."

"Fitever! Noo, tell me, I know something's going on and I don't know what it is."

Dod's rabbit-in-the-headlights expression didn't help his cause at all. He looked over at Grumphy, as if for advice but, seeing him conked out on the Grumphy leather chair, his heart sank.

"Da look at him for onyhin. He's lost in a world far the Dons are winning the Champions league. Look at him there, his little wee legs near kicking in his sleep. Noo, fit's gan on?"

Kylie moved in for the kill. She knew Dod was incapable of lying, and if he ever somehow did, he'd feel compelled to grass himself off. He cleared his throat. It seemed a prelude to a confession. At least, that's how it looked to Grumphy who, with one eye open and still imitating snoring, despaired at Dod. Didn't Dod even ken how to feign sleep when a wifie was interrogating him? That poor country Echt loon was mincemeat in the big city. Grumphy couldn't let that big lump of Dod take the fall. Not that Grumphy was morally opposed to such an event. It was just that he couldn't trust Dod not have them all done for. So, in time honoured fashion, Grumphy made out he was stirring as if he'd really been asleep the whole time, as opposed to carefully studying the scene under the guise of slumber.

"Yawn," said Grumphy.

"Granda! I knew if I put pressure on Dod I'd smoke you out. No one snores like that when they are actually sleeping."

Grumphy, sensing he'd been rumbled and tricked out into the open, tried to scurry back under the cover of pretend sleep, and started his ridiculous snoring. But he was forgetting Kylie had studied him at close quarters for 24 years. He'd been caught in a sting, a sting that was beyond even the conception of Dod.

"C'mon Granda. Do you really want to leave the spilling of the beans to Dod? It could mean the difference between 20 to life or the Death Penalty."

Dod looked at her and then at Grumphy. "But, but he's sleeping."

At this point Grumphy, realising just how naïve Dod was, opened his eyes and sat up, knowing the game was up. He looked at Dod and said, "da say another word, Dod, you'll get us all hanged."

"'All'? Fa's 'all'?

Grumphy realised he'd made as much a mess of this as he feared Dod might. At this point Mither came back into the room. Kylie, who'd up until now been simply curious as to what was going on, now had a sense that something pretty heavy was afoot. She was still kneeling beside Dod when she looked up at Mither and said, "'All'? Does this include you, Grandma?"

Mither initially had no idea what was going on but she

surveyed the devastation; Dod in shock, Grumphy obviously rumbled about something. She'd known Dod was going to try and talk to Grumphy about Kylie's father at the football. Dorothy had told her. So she hadn't given them a hard time for getting boozy or being late for supper as she'd surmised that the delicate chat may have been the cause. How much did Kylie know, if anything? Mither looked at Grumphy, trying to work out what had been said. But then, she decided to bank of womanly common sense. And tell the truth. At least, as much as she felt she could say in Dorothy's absence.

"Kylie, sweetheart. Come here."

Kylie looked up at Mither and looked more like a child than she'd done in a long time. For once, her bravado was gone. "Why?"

"Just come here, quine."

Kylie simply stood up and walked over to her Grandma, who put her arms around her. "What's happened, Grandma? Grumphy looked up at Mither. He had every faith she would handle this. Dod felt a little helpless. And responsible, seeing as the skeleton that was beginning to drop it bones out the cupboard had been disturbed by him in the first place. He stood up too. Kylie was leaning into her Grandma's chest. "Kylie," he said. "Come here."

"Jeez, mak up yer minds," said Kylie, with something like humour. Her Grandma let her go, and motioned her to go to Dod. She wasn't a child anymore. She was about to become a wife. And Dod was her husband-to-be. She did as she was bid and held onto Dod, who held her. "Quine, you know I love you very much."

"Yes."

Grumphy looked at Mither and motioned for them to leave the room. Mither overcame her instinctive reluctance to leave Kylie. Everything was now in Dod's hands. Mither and Grumphy left the room.

"Quine, maybe I should have told you first, but I wanted to tell you after I'd sounded everyone else out."

"About what?"

"I think I know where your mum has gone just now, and who she's meeting."

"How would you know? What's all this got to do with you?"

"Do you remember when you asked who would give you away?"

"Aye, but that's Grumphy's job. I was just thinking out loud."

"But you wouldn't have said it unless it was on your mind."

"I said it. I got it off my chest. It doesn't matter now."

"Actually, it might."

Kylie stood back a bit to look at Dod.

"Dod, I know you've always got the best of intentions. But please, tell me, what have you done?"

Dod took a deep breath.

"I asked your mum about your dad, your father, I mean."

Kylie's mouth was open but no words were coming out. Dod took this to mean something less than full approval.

"I just felt that you think about him sometimes."

"Eh, I don't even know who he is! How could I think about him?!"

"You know what I mean. Honey, I know you. But I know you have this big brave front."

"Oh, and I'm some shrinking violet behind this façade? Is that it? Have you been reading psychology on the internet again?"

"Eh?"

"Aye, I checked your history. I'd have been more relieved

to find porn there. But you've been checking out how children cope with missing parents."

"Why didn't you say you knew what I was checking out?"

"Why didn't you tell me? Dod, this bravado isn't an act. It's the real me. What you see is what you get. I'm not all sweet and soft in the middle you know."

"I'm not saying you are."

"I've had to be tough. What else should I do? Greet aboot my lost daddy? No. That's his loss. It's not mine. I've got all the family I need. And if you want to join it then you'd better respect that. Don't ever do shit like this behind my back again. Do you hear me?!"

"I do hear you, and I do respect that. But if you respect me then you'd better listen for once."

Kylie's mouth once again fell open. She was used to being the princess everyone tiptoed around. She was still mentally deciding on which verbal weapon to point in Dod's direction when he added,

"Respect is a two way street. Yes, I should have respected your privacy on this. But it isn't just your privacy anymore. It's *our* privacy. Your story is my story and my story is yours. We are together."

"Not yet! Don't count your chickens, min!"

"Aye, we are. We are together. So, we don't have a bit of paper to tell us yet. So what? We're together alright. And that means that we have to share things. We have to trust each other with our deepest hopes and fears. And I don't care what you say. I *know* you think about your father. I know how much you wonder about it. When you disappear into a wee world of your own and then someone calls you back and you return immediately with all your Kylie guns blazing, like you are embarrassed to even think about your dad."

59

"Father, actually."

"Ok, 'Father'."

"Dod, much as I respect your Engineering degree, I can't see how it qualifies you to be my therapist."

"I'm not your therapist. I'm your partner. I love you and want your happiness more than anything. That's my qualifications."

Kylie sat down. Dod knelt down beside her. He held her hand and she didn't take it away as he feared she might. "Honey, I was only asking about him, your father I mean. I just wanted to know if he was a good guy or a bad guy. If he was a bad guy I would have dropped it. As it happens, it was only today I asked Grumphy about him. Then I was going to tell you that I had. I didn't realise you'd get to this bit before I had told you all about it. I didn't really do anything wrong, darling. But I'm sorry if I went about this in a clumsy way. I've never experienced this situation before."

Kylie stroked his face. Dod continued. "Maybe I should have told you that I was checking out these things on the internet. But then, maybe you should have told me that your father was more on your mind than you said out loud. Trust is a two way street too."

Kylie leant forward and kissed him on the forehead and Dod kissed her hand. "What did he say?"

Dod looked at her. "Who?"

"Grumphy. What did Grumphy say about my father?"

"Well, he didn't appear to hate him, or think him the worst. But he said he broke your mum's heart. I don't think he'll ever forgive that."

"What else?"

"That was it."

"Are you sure?"

"Yes. It didn't seem a good idea to push Mr B on the issue. He did say that I should speak to you about it, though. I was going to do that tonight."

"Dod, I'm sorry."

"What for? Don't be silly."

"Well. Anyway. Do everything with me first from now on."

Dod smiled, replying, "Only if you share your thoughts with me. Deal?"

Kylie stood up and Dod followed. She put her arms around him and said, "Deal." She added, "So, you'd better tell me fa kens fit aboot this, just so we can all get on the same page."

Uphill Backwards

Pat watched from the Sainsbury Café as Dorothy drove away. He went to sip his tea. It was freezing. He hadn't touched it while meeting Dorothy. "Some way to wet the baby's head," he muttered to himself as he drank the cold tea.

Pat had no idea what to do now; where to go, who to call, what to say, what to think. He was lost in every sense. He knew what he *wanted* to do, which was to see his daughter right away. Dorothy had said that she'd need to prepare the ground and Pat had agreed. All being well he'd meet her the following day, but only after he'd met Mither and Grumphy. Then he'd meet his daughter. Dorothy had had it all mapped out. She'd tell him a little bit at a time. "Bite size portions", Dorothy had told him. And he'd have to go at her pace when it came to meeting *her* family. Pat didn't really have a choice here. He caught a glimpse of himself in the reflection in the café window. He looked, as Dorothy would have said years ago, a right mink. Hell, she'd have said it today if she hadn't been being polite.

Pat sensed a presence moving towards him. He turned round and there was Willie. Willie stopped. He looked a bit sheepish. Then he put his hand out and did the thumbs up sign, as if asking if all was ok. Pat beckoned him over.

"Right," said Pat, "what's next?"

Willie sat down and shrugged his shoulders and said, "That's up to you, mate."

"Oh, that's brilliant advice. Real wisdom there, pal."

Willie sighed, then asked, "Would you have come today if I'd told you what it was really all about?"

"Of course!"

"Really?"

"Aye. Eventually."

Willie laughed and said, "I thought *I* was the great procrastinator."

"You are, and you've got two votes for that, mine and Dorothy's."

"Well, you're here now. How's the whole 'got a secret daughter' thing for you? Good?"

Pat's cup of tea was on the way to his mouth when he pulled it away, looked at Willie quizzically, and then completed the gulping of the cold tea operation. He put the cup down on the table and said, "Aye. It could be worse, I suppose."

"Are you going to see her?"

"Tomorrow. After I've seen Grumphy, apparently."

"Ha ha! Good luck with that." Willie suddenly wished he hadn't put it exactly that way.

"Well, if he's got a shotgun, it'll have 25 years of rust jamming it."

"Ha ha. A shotgun? What'd he need that for? It's not you that's getting married."

Pat, who'd been staring out the window, suddenly looked Willie. "What do you mean, 'getting married'? Who's getting married?"

"You mean she didn't tell you?"

"Aye, she told me. That's why I'm asking you! You daft lump! Of course she didn't tell me."

"Oh."

"'Oh'? Is that it?"

Willie looked around and then back at Pat. "Aye."

"Unbelievable."

"I just thought she would have said."

"No, I'm being fed 'bite-sized' portions, apparently, like a flipping child."

"I can't tell you if she didn't tell you. It wouldn't be right."

"Hang on! Whose best pal are you? Hers or mine?"

"You don't need to ask that."

"Good. So …?" Pat did the rolling gesture with his hands again.

"See if you can work it out. That way I can truthfully say I didn't tell you."

"If I don't work it out in 30 seconds I'm going to introduce you to East German interrogation techniques I was trained in, Willie."

"Well, I've already told you earlier that Dorothy wasn't getting married."

"No you didn't."

"Yes I did!"

"No, you told me she *wasn't* married, not that she wasn't *getting* married. But you have now. Willie, you're really shite at this."

Pat was thinking that Willie might actually have survived a Cold War interrogation behind enemy lines because, in all likelihood, the interrogators would have blown their own brains out. If there'd been a whole army of Willies then The West would have reached Moscow within a week, trampling over the suicided Red Army, those badly injured but still breathing heard moaning "make him shut up or finish me off, I beg you."

"Well, I guess you can figure it out from here," said Willie.

Pat did indeed figure it out. "So, that's the big 'why now'?"

After his usual pause, Willie said, "Aye". Then adding, "No shotguns involved, by the way. All proper and above board. She's a good girl from what I can gather."

"Sensitive, Willie, real sensitive."

"I didn't mean –."

"What a perfect day. First I meet the old love of my live, then I find I've a daughter, and then, as an added bonus, I find out she's not up the duff. F*****g poetry, man, poetry."

"Like you said. It could be worse."

Next Morning

Grumphy and Mither were the only one's up, both sipping their cuppies. Grumphy was a coffee man, Mither strictly tea. There was a cafeteria unused by the sink with a slight crack in it, a result of Grumphy's inability to work out how to use it. The last time he tried he'd put unground coffee beans into it and covered them with boiling water, left it for 5 minutes then pressed down "the thingy" and poured out the resulting slightly discoloured water into his mug. He couldn't see what all the fuss about real coffee was, apparently, as it "just tasted like dishwater".

Mither had pointed out that that was effectively what he was drinking, suggesting that instead of adding milk he should add Fairy Liquid and make a start on washing the dishes. Grumphy had picked up the cafeteria, realised his error, and replaced it on the kitchen top with just a tad of temper. It had sat there ever since, a monument to Grumphy's distaste for "gadgets". "What time did they go to bed?" asked Grumphy.

He was referring Kylie and her mum, who, after Dorothy had returned, talked all night. Dorothy had been relieved Kylie was very matter of fact about the situation, although she realised that was partly for show. She was even more relieved Kylie had supported her in every way. Kylie had felt for her mum and the choices she'd been forced to make. Kylie had asked a million questions. It had been an emotional discussion but it was between a mother and daughter who were each other's best friends. There would be more discussions to be had on the matter. That was for sure. But life would go on.

"About 4am," replied Mither.

"Well?"

"Well what?"

"Well, you'd have been listening at the door a night or you'll have disgraced your sex's reputation for 'overhearing' things."

Mither put her hand on his across the table. "They're fine, George."

"Sounds too easy to me."

"Well, what I should say is they *will* be fine."

"Ach, the poor quines. What a shock for the wee een."

"Well, it's not like she didn't know she had a dad."

"Father."

"Aye, indeed. Father."

Grumphy supped a bit more. "I take it you kent oor Dot was gan ti meet *The Father*." Grumphy said *The Father* the same way he said *Football*, with distaste and sarcasm.

"Aye. I did, George. I just thought —."

"Da worry aboot nae telling me. I ken you're the best judge of these things." He patted her hand, an unusual display of affection for Grumphy.

"Jesus! Get a room, you two!" Kylie had stormed in.

Grumphy and Mither looked at her and then at each other. There'd been no visible red eye, no tear-stained cheeks, no sign of anything other than Kylie as her normal self.

"Ha ha. That's so cute! So yoos were sitting there thinking I'd be swept up in the drama? What do you take me for?" Kylie smiled at them and asked if they wanted another cuppy.

"We're fine, quine. Glad to see you are tae, by the sound o it?" Grumphy was only partly convinced.

"Da worry aboot me. You two lovebirds can get your glad

67

rags looked out. We're gan for supper the night."

"What's the occasion?" asked Grumphy out of habit and without thinking.

Mither and Kylie looked at him. It gradually dawned on Grumphy

"Wild guess? A long lost relative?"

A real smile beamed over Kylie's face. "Aye. And ye ken fine fa it is."

Grumphy and Mither were both a bit taken aback by Kylie's apparent easy adjustment to what must have been a shock. Kylie recognised this and sat down at the table with them. She put one of her hands on each of theirs'. "Da worry, ok? I ken it'll take a while to take everything in. But can't you see? It's nae the big shock to me that you might think. I always kent I had a father, and that for her own good reasons Ma didna want him aroon. And if she didna, then I didna. But now that she think's it's time, then I think it's time too."

Grumphy went to counsel caution, "Quine -."

"Granda, dinna worry. I've nae got great hopes aboot him. Meeting my father will not change anything between us all, I swear. This is just something I have to do. I am part of him. 50% of me in fact. That big lump of Dod got one thing right. I've always wondered about my father. Don't get me wrong. I havna lain awake greetin' every night a these years. But, I've always wanted this day to come."

Grumphy and Mither could see clearly why such a smile was on Kylie's face, brightening up the room. They just prayed it wouldn't disappear as suddenly as it seemed to have come along. As for her father, he could disappear anytime he liked, thought Grumphy.

Still, for reasons Grumphy and Mither could only part

grasp, Kylie had a definite spring in her step. She got up from the table.

"Far are you gan, Quine?" asked Mither

"Bane the hoose to spik ti Ma. We've got a lot to spik aboot! Then I'm awa to spik to Dod. This is all his doing and, for once, I might just tell him he's done something right!"

Mither went to say something but stopped. Kylie read her mind. "Come awa bane, Grandma."

"Aye, awa bane ti wifie central," said Grumphy. "Jist gie me the highlights efter."

Grumphy drained his cuppy, muttering to himself, "You already broke een o ma quine's hairts. If you brak anither een, I'll f*****g kill you."

Grumphy wanted to alert Dod, so he pulled out his mobile phone. This showed he meant business. He hated using it. He often "got a hud o some wifie fa I da even ken and fa telt me yon number wisna recognised." Dod in particular had wanted to take a photo of Grumphy's face while Kylie explained that it wasn't a wifie at all but an automatic computer "fa sounded like a wifie".

Dod had incurred Kylie's wrath at the time when Grumphy had gotten his first ever mobile phone, an iPhone no less. Dod had shown Grumphy how to take pictures and send them to his friends and family. Except Dod had deliberately told Grumphy that "this wee button here" took a photo of whatever Grumphy pointed the phone at. So, when Grumphy's family and friends soon received numerous extreme close-up photos of Grumphy's face in various states of confusion and intensity, it was apparent that Grumphy had received somewhat poor instruction from Dod. Dod took the beating from Kylie as it was worth it. Plus he had one compensation. Suffice to say that whenever Dod received a call from Grumphy a picture of Grumphy's face red with frustration came up on Dod's phone. That and the theme tune from Laurel and Hardy ringing as Grumphy's caller ID.

Half as Nice

Kylie had half a mind she wanted to meet her father on her own. She'd had so many personal thoughts about him over the years that she felt strangely close to him even though she didn't know him. She'd harboured hopes all her life that he was a good guy. The fact that he was never spoken about at all meant that his reputation had been nurtured in some neutral cold storage. The past was about to thaw out. Kylie had no idea what really lay under all this frozen time. But instinct was encouraging her to have a look.

Now she found herself wondering what her father would make of her. Would he be proud? Would he be cold? Aloof? Would they click? Would he just say, "Nice to meet you, goodbye?" Should she try to impress? Should she play it cool? Her mother had always told her to just be herself. But who was she? Really? It wasn't just her father coming out from under the ice of time. It was part of her too. 50% of her in fact.

Here she was, in Dod's arms as they lay on his bed.

"Remember you said meeting your father wouldn't change anything between us all?"

"Yes, and it's true."

"Don't let it change you either."

Kylie sat up on the bed. "I ken I'm perfect already, so why should I change?" She was laughing.

"But you are perfect. Perfect for me, just as you are."

"You've been reading psychology online again?"

"Ha ha. No, I've just been reading your mind again."

"Well, you're better at that than I thought you were. But, what if you only ken part of me?"

"You mean 50% of you?" He laughed. Kylie was almost obsessing about this unknown half of her.

"We can laugh, but what if I have a dark side?"

"Ha ha, it's the dark side I already know! I'm kinda hoping the other 50% is human."

"You're still nae as funny as Grumphy – and he's nae funny at a."

"Come here," and Dod pulled her back down onto the bed. "See, whatever parts of you exist, known and unknown, I love them all, no matter what, forever."

Kylie's heart warmed to Dod's words. He was the only boyfriend who'd ever stood up to her and the only one she'd really respected and trusted. Thank goodness it was his arms she was in, she thought.

"Maybe, just maybe, the other 50% of you is the soppy side that's been hiding away."

Kylie bolted up. "Da get your hopes up. It's Mither fa reads Mills and Boon books, nae me."

"Ha ha. Aye, you're the only girl I ever dated who named *Jaws* as her favourite book."

"Aye, and *The Godfather* as my favourite film."

"Wonder what your dad's favourite film is."

"Father, not dad."

"Not yet. But you never know."

"True. You never know. All I do know is who my husband will be and how long I'll be his wife."

"Ha ha. You've been reading Mither's Mills and Boon books on the fly!"

"Wise up!"

"I'll break through your thick skin one day."

"Aye, well, you're getting sweet eff all until our wedding night."

The Hunger

"*La Tasca*? Why *La Tasca*?" Grumphy wasn't keen on eating in "fancy" restaurants when nothing "could beat a chipper".

"George. You can hae something simple. Besides, we're hardly gan for the food. There's mair important things to think aboot tonight!" Mither had moments of great impatience with Grumphy. Here they were, all about to meet their granddaughter's father for the first time in 25 years, and Grumphy was thinking of the food.

"But it's nae the food I'm thinking aboot," he said, reading her mind. "It's my stomach. Jist think. You'll all be playing Families Reunited and I'll be stuck in the lavvy a night."

"That's why I said just hae something simple."

"It's nae the food, I keep trying to tell you. It's my nerves. I jist hope this clown is for real and nae gan tae cause us a hairtburn."

"Nerves? You?"

"Aye, coz I da ken fit a might dae if *The Father* gives aff any bad vibes."

"Da, I ken fit you'll dae."

"Aye, George, so do I."

"Aye? Fit?"

"F*** all!" It was not often George heard his wife and daughter swear in unison. So, he took this to be a wee clipping of his wings.

They entered *La Tasca,* and were escorted to a table right at the back. Dorothy had booked it earlier and requested as much privacy as possible. She'd explained that it was a delicate family matter.

Dorothy, Mither and Grumphy were first to arrive. The menus were delivered. Grumphy looked at his, then looked at Mither, then back at the menu, then back at Mither.

"Fit, George!"

"I da spik Polish, so I've nae idea fits on this menu."

"It's Spanish, Da, nae Polish!"

"But the waitress sounded Polish?"

"How would you ken, George. You just said you da spik Polish."

Mither had him there, nae doot, Grumphy thought to himself.

The waitress came over and said, "Hi. Is everything alright?"

Grumphy looked up, "Well, I'm a bit concerned aboot the political situation in Caracas at the moment. But apart fae that ..."

The waitress looked puzzled.

"Don't worry about my father. He's in a funny mood."

The waitress smiled and walked away, murmuring to herself, "you could have fooled me".

"I still da ken why we couldna jist hae a met at oor ain place."

"George, it's better we all met in a public place. And this is where Kylie and Dod met. This is their favourite place. It's where Kylie feels secure. It's her choice, and that's the way it should be."

"I thought they met at *Drummonds*."

"No, they went there after their meal the night they met. But this is where they actually first met. You must remember? They both were on Christmas nights out? Mind he bumped into her and she'd given him an earful? And he sent over a bottle of champagne to her table?"

75

"It was over a year ago, woman. I canna mind fit happened last wik, never mind last year."

"Never mind, George."

"Then fits *Drummonds* got ti dae wi it?"

Dorothy sighed. "Da, they went there to watch a band play later on that night. Dod asked her. How many times have you heard this story and forgotten it?"

"Aye, aye, fitever. Noo, far is love's young dream onywy?"

"I da ken. Why not text them?" said Dorothy, looking at Mither discreetly. She knew she'd created a few minutes of mirth as Grumphy's bumbling fingers hit the phone keypad in what looked like random fashion. Mither looked at Dorothy, chiding her a little for her mischievousness. Still, Mither couldn't deny it was fun. Eventually, Grumphy said, "Bingo."

At that point, on Union Street just beside the Cooperative, the theme tune to Laurel and Hardy played. It was on Dod's phone. He and Kylie had just had a couple of quick drinks in *Drummonds* and were walking up to meet the rest. Dod took out his phone from his pocket and the Laurel and Hardy theme tune played louder. He showed the phone to Kylie and they both burst out laughing as Grumphy's face appeared on the screen, peering into it out at them. He'd Facetimed them without knowing it. Grumphy went to speak but somehow cut the phone off.

"We're being summoned," said Dod. "How are you doing, honey?"

Kylie was nervous. She had enough gumption to hide it. But not enough to hide it from Dod. Didn't stop her trying though. "I'll be okay. Da worry aboot me."

"You will be fine. Remember, if anyone has to impress, it's him, not you."

"I know. But that's easier to say than think."

Dod knew that saying too much now would just cloud Kylie's mind. Besides, she would actually be fine. He was certain of that. But now it was time for him to simply be there in the background, there if needed.

Dod held the *La Tasca* door open for Kylie as she walked in. He quickly walked beside her and took her hand. It wasn't often she squeezed his hand but she did at that moment. The waitress escorted them over to join Dorothy, Mither and Grumphy. Kylie was relieved that it was only them there. She was now very keen to meet her father, but was also dreading it more than she had imagined she would. She had always known that her dad didn't know about her so she knew he hadn't rejected her. Mercifully she'd never felt that at all. But, she feared now there'd be plenty of time for him to do that now. She'd never expected to have this fear. Suddenly, despite being in the familiar *La Tasca*, she was entering the unknown.

Dressing for Dinner

"You can't meet anyone like that!"

Willie was rarely as forthright as this, thought Pat.

"Like what?"

"Like someone who's fallen out a bin liner. I've seen dismembered bodies that looked more together!"

"When?" challenged Pat.

"It's a figure of speech. But seriously. This is your daughter you're going to meet."

"Well, it's all I've got. I have shaved though. Here, look." Pat drew attention to his chin. He had indeed shaved. But he seemed to have taken off as much skin as stubble.

"Jeez, where'd you get the razor?"

"Hotel issue."

"Deadly."

Pat had spent the night at The Copthorne Hotel on Huntly Street. Willie had put it through as some kind of business expense and would settle the bill. It was lunchtime and they were sitting in the bar with chips and burgers. No beer. Pat had said he was too nervous for beer. In a weird way that computed, thought Willie.

"Well, like I said. You can't go like that." Willie was firm and Pat, shattered from a night of no sleep and no alcohol, was happy to follow orders, a most unusual circumstance. "Finish that, and we'll go over the road and get you something to wear that won't have folk throwing change at you in the street."

Within the hour Willie had Pat kitted out at Slaters. He

also insisted Pat go back to his hotel room and get a rest. He'd call in for him around 6pm, an hour before Pat had to be at *La Tasca* to meet his daughter, and Dorothy, and Mither, and Grumphy, and whoever else this new family might consist of.

Family. That might be pushing it, thought Pat. But he'd resolved to stay in Aberdeen, for a while at least. He had a daughter to get to know. And bridges to repair. He had these to repair all over the world. But let's start with Aberdeen, he thought.

"Open up! It's the Child Support Agency!" The pounding on Pat's hotel room echoed in his head. He'd dozed off just a few moments before. He was dressed and ready to go. He opened the door to ask the door knocker what they were playing at.

"Oh, it's you. That's real funny, Willie."

"My God, you're actually ready."

Soon they were walking down the cobbles of Huntley Street when Willie went to say something and Pat put his hand up and said, "Don't say anything Willie. I'm getting into the zone."

"Shiteing it, are we?"

"I don't know about you but I am."

"You'll be fine. How wrong could it go? I mean, I guess the worst it could get would be if Grumphy went for you, or if Dorothy went for you, or if Mither went for you, or if her fiancé went for you. Actually, the more I think about it, I can't see you getting out alive."

"What's this? Tough love?"

"Without the love".

"You're all heart. What time are they expecting us?"

"Us? Pat, I hope you've not got the wrong end of the stick, mate. They're only expecting you."

79

"Eh!?"

"She's not my daughter. It's not me Grumphy's brought his shotgun for."

"Funny stuff, Willie, you're cracking me up. But seriously -."

"But seriously, it's your gig, pal. Look, there it is. *La Tasca*. You like Tapas?"

Pat looked at him with some astonishment. "Aye, I like Tapas, which is why I'm going to *La Tasca* of course. The fact that my long lost daughter who I never knew I had until yesterday will be there is just a wee bonus. Sure, I might have a wee blether with her, if there's time, like."

"Jeez, I just asked."

"Muppet."

Willie smiled. "I suggest a quick pint and or wee brandy. We're right across the road. Even you can't get out of this now."

"Funny thing is, I don't want out of this. I just want to go there right now. I need some chewing gum, Willie. Here, lets nip into this Coop and get some."

"I'll get it, Pat. You want anything else?"

"Na, that's it, Willie."

"Wait here, pal."

Just as Willie went into the Coop on Union Street, Pat could've sworn he'd just heard the Laurel and Hardy theme tune in his head. He looked around but no Laurel and Hardy, just a young couple walking passed, laughing. Pat smiled, thinking to himself, "Loves young dream."

Dinner is Served

"Ever jumped out a plane, Pat?"

"Aye, but not for while."

Willie opened the door at *La Tasca* and said, "Don't worry, it'll come back to you," and pushed Pat through the door. Willie then walked away, but only a few doors along, to *The Justice Mill*, and went inside. He ordered a pint and a wee brandy, taking his phone out to make sure that should Pat call for back-up he could intervene if needed. But, Pat was Pat, he thought. He'd be fine. Willie put the phone on the bar just in front of him so he could see it anyway, just in case.

Pat landed in *La Tasca* and without a parachute. He was greeted by a waitress who asked if he had a reservation. He looked around and saw a lot of smartly dressed types who looked like they were in after work for a beer or a bite to eat. Suddenly he was glad he was better dressed than he was the day before.

"Aye, I think there this a reservation."

"What name, sir?"

Pat realised it would be in Dorothy's family name. "Buchan," he said.

"Ah, yes sir. Your family is sitting over this way. Come with me please."

Family? Yikes. What an imposter he felt.

Pat's steps from the front of the restaurant towards the table at the back of it were the most nerve-racking in a lifetime of nerve-racking steps. He was managing surging and conflicting emotions of anger, guilt and regrets. Nothing in his life had prepared Pat for this moment.

He saw Dorothy sitting facing in his direction. He assumed the older couple with their back to him were Mither and Grumphy. Then he saw her. His daughter, sitting beside some guy, at the end of the table. My God. He froze still. She was the double of Dorothy at that age. He could hear talking from the table. He spotted an empty seat beside Dorothy. It was a smaller table than he imagined. Scarily intimate. Dorothy looked up from the table as the waitress stood with menus in hand wondering whether to wait for Pat or to proceed to the table. Pat was trapped in no man's land. He caught Dorothy's eye. It was like he needed her permission, or at least encouragement, to move towards them. Dorothy smiled. Politely, not necessarily affectionately.

But these things only partly held Pat's attention. He looked back at the main focus. Kylie. She had looked up just after Dorothy smiled. She caught his gaze and looked, initially, quizzically. Then, as the moment dawned on her, a smile broke out on her face. "Oh my God. She's pleased to see me." Then Pat said to himself, like he was giving an order, "don't you dare blow this."

He smiled back without knowing it. Without thinking he put out his arms. Kylie, without waiting for a second, stood up and slowly walked towards him, her face staring at his. She was beautiful, Pat thought. The closer she got, the more he could see Kylie under the initial impression of Dorothy. Pat didn't know what to say, so he just let the first words that came into his head fall out his mouth.

"Hello Kylie, I'm your Dad."

"Father," she replied, somewhat defiantly. "Father for now. 'Dad' comes later."

Pat was a little wrong-footed but immediately understood. "Yes," he nodded, 'Dad' come's later."

Kylie took the remaining steps towards Pat. His arms were still open. Kylie allowed herself to walk into them despite all the voices in her head telling her to be careful. They were just her fears. For now, her hopes were winning. Pat put his arms around the daughter he didn't know he had until the previous day, feeling so very close to this child in his arms. He was overwhelmed. But he wasn't going to make an awkward situation any more awkward by giving in to the urge to cry. He just held her, and whispered without meaning to, "my daughter."

Kylie had her own steel. She wasn't going to cry either. She had the feelings of her family to consider, the same family who had loved her and made her who she was. How could she insult them by forgetting all about them just now, even though at his moment, all she could feel was the once-dormant love now filling her heart. Father was here. And 'Dad' was surely not far behind.

They both stood back to look at each other. Both their faces were radiant. Dorothy could see it plainly. She was pleased but apprehensive. Step one has gone well, she thought. But there's a lot steps to go. Dod, who'd stood up, when Pat arrived, could only look on, praying he'd done the right thing. It was obvious to everyone that Kylie was experiencing a life changing event right in front of their eyes. Would everything change? Dod had no choice but to have faith in Kylie's good sense.

Grumphy and Mither had both turned round. Mither was smiling, she could see that Kylie's happiness and her good sense were working hand in hand. Besides, whatever happened, Mither knew that Kylie had the strongest and most loving family in Aberdeen and they were always going to be there for Kylie, no matter what. At 68, she'd seen most dramas played out at one time or another. There was nothing that couldn't be fixed, or at least managed. That's what families were for.

Grumphy could see his granddaughter was as happy. This wrong-footed him. He might have to put the mental shotgun away, for now. Mither had told him about how Dorothy had mellowed towards Pat and if she could then Grumphy had better too. No one had any illusions. But, when they thought about it, what had Pat actually done wrong all these years ago? Apart from be young? He'd never deserted Dorothy. It had been Dorothy's choice, although Pat being so selfish a boyfriend had left her feeling she'd had no choice. Still, Grumphy had started to wonder how it would feel to be in Pat's shoes, like, just finding out he had a daughter he never knew about. This wasn't going to be easy, thought Grumphy. But if this is what his family wanted, then that had to count.

Kylie came over to the table, pulling her father by the hand. "Everyone, this is my father." Pat leant forward to shake Dod's hand. Dod, who was still standing, reciprocated.

"A pleasure to meet you, Mr …?"

"Pat, just plain, Pat."

"Pat." Dod smiled.

Mither stood up and turned round to greet Pat. "It's been a long time, Pat."

"Too long, Mrs B, too long."

They shook hands.

Pat went round to greet Grumphy, who was slow in getting up. But get up he did. He grasped Pat's hand with a very strong grip. Pat thought to himself, "Ok, I get it. You're daddy bear." But, out loud he said, "Mr B. You're looking well."

"As well as can be under the circumstances, I suppose."

"Anyway, you look well."

84

The tension between the two alpha males was obvious. Grumphy had been as much a dad and grandad to Kylie. And this whippersnapper, albeit a pretty old whippersnapper, was strolling in after the decades of hard parenting had been done. "I'll welcome the bugger," thought Grumphy, adding, "to a point."

Dorothy stood up. "Thanks for coming," was all she could think to say.

Pat smiled at her with a newfound gratitude. "Wouldn't have missed it for the world."

"Sit down, Pat," and she motioned for him to sit in the empty chair next to her.

The waitress, who'd sensed a delicate scene and stepped back to the bar, came over again, and said innocently, "so, all the family's here?"

Pat looked at Dorothy and he still had his smile beaming. Dorothy answered the waitress, "yes, all here."

Everyone ordered light Tapas and drinks. Pat had requested tap water. There was too much going on inside him to risk alcohol.

"Tap water, Patrick? What a pleasant surprise. Are you a reformed man?" Grumphy well remembered the 1980s version of Pat.

"No, Mr B, I've just grown up a bit."

"What, in the last 24 hours? From what Oor Dot said, you looked wasted this time yesterday."

Dorothy's mouth dropped open. Mither's elbows tried to jab Grumphy's ribs but missed. Kylie knew Grumphy had to get some stuff off his chest. He had to assert himself a little bit. She'd been reading psychology on the internet.

Pat coughed nervously. "Well, it'd been a long day."

"A long month, I'd heard, Patrick."

"Aye, something like that."

"You're looking snappily dressed, Patrick. I'll say that for you."

"Mr B, just call me Pat."

Grumphy sensed an opportunity to test Pat. "But Patrick's your name?"

"Aye, but you can just use the shortened version."

Grumphy looked at him, thinking, and said, "You mean, 'Rick'?"

"No."

"But that's a shortened version?"

"No! It starts with a 'P'!"

Grumphy paused only for a moment before saying, "Prick?"

Dod ventured, "I think we're getting off on the wrong foot here, chaps."

"Da worry, Dod, Pat's nae prickly."

Pat went to say something, but actually couldn't prevent a laugh coming out instead. Well, Grumphy hadn't changed, that was for sure.

"No, but I am bit rickly," ventured Pat.

Grumphy laughed despite himself.

The waitress appeared with the drinks. She dished them out and was left with just the tap water on the tray. She looked around, trying to see who didn't have a drink beside them. Grumphy caught her eye and said, "Oh, that's for Rick here.

The table laughed, some members of it more nervously than others. Kylie lent over and whispered to Dod, "this is all your doing, so, you might have to be the referee between these two." She was still smiling though.

Post-Match Analysis

Willie was on his fourth pint. He'd been checking his phone. No call or text from Pat. Either Grumphy's already had him unconscious in the boot of a car heading off the cliffs at Torry, or everything had passed off peacefully. He decided to step outside and get some fresh air. Snow was falling. A figure in a suit nearly slipped on the pavement just outside *La Tasca*. Was that Pat? Poor Weegies shouldn't be let out on their own in the Northern snow. And, man, thought Willie, new shoes and snow just do not go together.

"Pat?"

The figure in the suit in the snow stopped and turned round. Willie ran up to him. "Pat, don't keep me in suspense. Where's everyone else? How'd it go?"

"They all left together about 10 minutes ago. I think it went well. I'm a bit dazed, mate. But, aye, it went well, I suppose. But, not being a veteran of such events, I don't know for sure.

"Any fights?"

"Ha ha. No."

"Well, that's a result. How about your daughter, how'd you get on?"

"Like a house on fire, Willie. She's amazing. Very like her mum. Very smart, very strong, very …"

"… very Dorothy."

"Aye."

"The big question. Grumphy?"

"He was actually ok, after doing his 'man of the tribe' act

to start with. I don't think we'll be buddies anytime soon, but the atmosphere ended up fine. And her fiancé, Dod, what a decent lad he seems. A bit posh, but decent."

"Posh but decent. Aye, Could be worse."

"Mither was more welcoming than the last time I seen her. And Dorothy was yon controlled way but I think she was OK. But I gotta say, Kylie is something else. Apart from Grumphy I think she runs the show!"

"You sound proud, Pat."

"Aye, I am. And I think she liked me."

"You'd have to blow it pretty spectacularly for her not to. She's part of you, for goodness sake. But, then again, I suppose there's plenty of time for any disappointment to come through."

Pat stopped slithering along the pavement for long enough to register a disapproving look at Willie. "Mr, Motivator, eh?"

"So, what's next, Pat?"

"A drink."

They headed to *The Stag*. Willie seemed to know the lads behind the bar and soon two beers were heading over in his hands.

"What's this?"

"Lager, why?"

"When I said a drink, I meant like, an actual drink."

Willie smiled. "These are just to dilute what's coming." He disappeared and then reappeared with two large brandies.

"Ah, said Pat, "Now, I understand. How could I have doubted you?"

Willie put a brandy in Pat's hand, and then clinked glasses. "To your daughter!"

Pat's couldn't help but beam back, "To my daughter!"

Pat recounted the evening with pride and joy. Willie kept

him company as the brandies flowed, watered down with lager. Pat couldn't wait to see Kylie again. Willie knew there were a lot of practical issues to consider, like a job, somewhere to live, razor blades that left some skin on the face, and shoes that didn't act as banana skins when it snowed. There'd by enough banana skins ahead, Willie was sure of that.

Dorothy had apparently suggested that Pat, Grumphy and Dod spend some time together the following evening. This would give the quines a chance to regroup and the mannies a chance to bond. Well, Dorothy wasn't as unrealistic as to think the men would be Walking The Mat arm in arm anytime soon. But it was another step, another bite-sized portion.

"You'll be looking forward to that, Pat."

"Aye, oh aye. Being called 'Rick' all night. Wonder how many times he'll tell that 'prick' joke before he tires of it."

"He'll not tire of it this side of the Dons winning the Champions League."

"Next year then!"

Willie wasn't convinced.

The Rosemount Summit

Back at the flat Kylie was on a high. But she knew she had to be sensitive to the feelings of all.

"Granda, you're still geing me awa, at my wedding, I mean."

Grumphy knew when to be philosophical, or at least when to feign being philosophical."

"Quine, fitever you want is fitever I want."

Mither looked over at Grumphy, unconvinced.

"Well, that's just as well, Granda. So, da think that'll change. It is what I've always wanted."

Grumphy said to Kylie, "That's settled then." But to himself he said, "Phew!"

"So," said, Dorothy, "far are you gan the morn's night? You know, for your lad's night out?"

Dorothy could speak as Doric as anyone but she tried to speak "properly", just as Mither did sometimes. Grumphy spoke like Grumphy and that was that. Kylie knew how to speak however it suited her and she found it fascinating that they all seemed to speak Doric more when they were tired or stressed. Tonight there was plenty of tiredness and stress to go round. But also much relief.

"I'll organise it if you like, Mr B."

Now, Grumphy knew Dod was always helpful but, he thought, fit could a poor loon fae Echt, even a posh but decent een like Dod, possibly know about a night out in the big city? Jeez, that big lump of Dod would have us all at a rugby match or something just as weird, thought Grumphy.

"Nae bither, Dod. I'll get it organised. But da worry, I'll mak sure it's a venue where there's plenty of parking for your tractor."

"Are you sure now, George?" Mither knew it'd been a few years since her husband had had occasion to arrange any such nights out.

"Aye, I'm sure. Why wouldn't I be?"

"Nae strippers Granda, nae female ones onywy!" said Kylie. Mither and Dorothy laughed.

"Da you worry." Grumphy, now felt challenged.

"What have you got in mind, Granda? Nothing too wild I hope?"

Wild? thought Grumphy, as if that fermer's boy and the newly-returned Rick could honul a richt nicht oot. No, it would just hae to be a few wee drinkies in a sensible setting, one befitting gentlemen. Somewhere they could spick. There'd be a fair bit o' spicking to be done. I'll surprise them, thought Grumphy. Something mair classy than they'd think me capable o'. Grumphy was a veteran of a 100 staggers and this wouldn't even be a stagger, just a wee night out.

The League of Gentlemen

The next morning, Dod was lying in his bed. Echt was lit up by sunshine and the glare from overnight snow seemed to double the power of the light. He was feeling quite pleased with himself. The skeleton that he'd dragged out the Buchan's cupboard had turned out to be quite benign, and it had only drunk tap water. He'd actually liked Pat, on first impression anyway. Kylie obviously was delighted to have met him. She'd told Dod that while Grumphy would be giving her away, "nae doot", she wanted to find some role for her father and she wasn't keen on Grumphy's suggestion of making him a bridesmaid. Dod had suggested usher, but Kylie had wanted something a bit more for her father. But, she didn't know what.

Still, things were going in the right direction, thought Dod.

His phone started ringing. He didn't need to look to see who it was. It was Laurel and Hardy rolled into one Grumphy. He chuckled as their theme tune rang out in his room. He answered it. No voice. He looked at the phone. There was Grumphy, face right up close and personal to the screen as he clearly had Facetimed Dod by accident. Dod pressed the appropriate button and answered Grumphy's Facetime call. Grumphy jumped back from the screen, obviously surprised to see Dod's actual face on his own screen. "Hang up and I'll call you back, Mr B." Dod had no wish to add to his already considerable experience of talking Grumphy through the minefield of Facetime. Whether he intended to or not, Grumphy hung up. Dod called him.

"Dod, you'll need tae tak this bloody thing back tae the shoppie. Ah da ken fits wrang wi it."

Dod glossed over what had become a ritual. Most people said "hello" at the start of phone call. But Grumphy started with words like, "phone …shit …piece of …etc."

"Anyway, Mr B. Where are we off to tonight? Have you got something sorted?"

"Aye, I huv. And it's a classy joint tae."

Dod decided to have a bit of leg pull. "Let me guess, it's the rugby club at Aberdeen Wanderers?"

"Fit?"

"I hear they do an excellent Duck la Orange, and the maître d knows just how to keep folks in line."

There was a pause, followed by, "Dod, will you no just get me a proper phone next time. I've got some French bugger wi a cross line here."

Don't do anything else that might prolong this call, thought Dod.

"Onywy, I've booked the three of us into this place."

"What place?"

"Never you mind. Let's just say that when I booked I was thinking somewhere for someone like you. Somewhere that welcomed proper gents. You've already been to *The Stag*, so ah didna want to push oor luck by takking you there twice in a week. Noo, you're better wi phones than I am. So you're gonna call Rick tell him far we're meeting. Kylie'll gie you his number. Noo, the message is we meet at Bridge Street at 10pm. Dress smart."

"10pm? Is that not a bit late."

Grumphy smiled to himself. Ach that poor country loon. Didn't he ken that sometimes the best places didn't open until late at night? Grumphy hoped that Dod's search for a city place would get him out of Echt ASAP. He didn't want his granddaughter moving miles away or, for that matter, centuries back in time.

Truth be told, Grumphy himself was a little surprised that the place he'd booked didn't take bookings before 10pm. Ach, well. It was the modern world. Best just try and keep up, he'd thought. Besides, he couldn't be more modern. He'd even used the internet, and that wasn't something that happened every day. Grumphy was pleased it had all been so simple. All he'd had to do was type into something called a search engine the words, "Gentleman's Club". Technology wasn't so bad after all.

Set Up

Pat woke up and, as he went to get out of bed, he realised he was in agony. He managed to sit up. Then he spotted the new shoes kicked off beside the chair in his hotel room. I'd have fallen less wearing Vaseline on the soles of these bastard things, he thought to himself. His knew suit seemed to have dried out. He'd had the sense to hang it up in the room. Just as well, because he really did not have any other clothes. The rags he'd been wearing in Glasgow were okay for the Debbie's of the world, but not when family were around. Mental note – get high powered job ASAP so I can buy clothes, car, and loads of other shit. I can't take Kylie out looking like a mink.

Wait, what was he thinking? Take Kylie out? She wasn't four years old. What was he going to do? Take her to the park, buy her ice cream? Go to the pictures? Try and cram twenty-five years-worth of good parenting into the four months before she got married? Mmm. Good point. So, how exactly should a long lost father go about coming into the life of a child who was not a child but a woman?

There was no one he could call to get the answers. Willie wouldn't have a clue. Grumphy would just call him "Prick" and laugh. Dod would be all posh but decent, smile, be polite and say nothing any import. Dorothy would map it all out in bite-sized steps or whatever she called the process. Mither would . . . would what? Mither. That might actually be a good call. Pat kept that thought to go back to.

He went to call Willie but before he could dial, a number called his phone.

"Hello? Dod? Yes, it's me. Aye, good to meet you last night too. Don't bother with the 'sir'. Just plain old 'Pat' will do. That's right. Yes, I agree, 'Prick' wasn't funny at all. Look, Dod, what do you want?"

Pat received Dod's news of the Rendezvous. He noted it down in his note book and called Willie, asking him to remind him where Bridge Street was. Willie gave him directions and told him they should meet for lunch at the best Thai in town, in *Aberdeen Market Village*. It was there at *Madame Mews* café, Pat was told to get a job by Willie, a job Willie had sorted out for him. It should be a formality. But he had to attend an interview set up especially for him. Willie had sounded out this firm a few weeks ago for Pat. It was perfect for him. Decent pay, and freedom to run Security his way. Security was Pat's forte and his CV (which Willie had created for him) emphasising his military record, minus the "bopping a Rupert in the face" bit, had gone down very well.

"You'll need another suit, mate. And a few other things too."

"Willie, it's been a whirlwind and I've not stopped to thank you for helping me out so much."

"You'd do the same for me."

"Maybe." Pat smiled.

"Anyway, these are high-powered guys. There's a bit of the Rupert about them. But please don't punch them, not until you get the job anyway. Company I work for needs their support from time to time. So, you'll have to behave."

"I know how to behave, Willie. I behaved for a long time."

"Well, good. Same again, please. Now, these guys love their golf. I may have let them believe you were something of a golfer too."

Pat looked at him. "'Let them believe'? How does that

occur, Willie? For instance, what might have given them the idea that I'm a golfer in the first place?"

"It might have been something I said."

"Aye, it might just have been."

"I may even have said that the first thing you did when you knew you were moving here was join a golf club, such was your obsession."

"Well, at least you didn't lay it on too thick! Jesus, Willie!"

"Anyway, these guys are officer class. They just want to approve you as their toy soldier. Indulge them. Talk golf. You've worked undercover before. I'm sure if you survived East Germany in the Cold War I dare say you'll cope with Holburn Street."

"I dunno Willie, which end of Holburn Street are we talking about?"

"Very funny. Pat, I'm serious. Good job. Freedom. Travel. Money. How long is up to you, assuming you survive a three month probationary period."

Pat knew this was something he couldn't blow. "I'll research this game you speak of. Golf, you call it? I hate golf. It's for -."

"It's for *you*. It is tomorrow anyway. 2pm. Admiral Court, down by the Fish Houses, behind Union Square."

"You're sounding like I have the faintest idea where you're talking about."

Willie smiled. He took a street map from his pocket and threw it over the table to Pat.

"Knock 'em dead, soldier – just not literally."

Building Bridges

"Another new suit, Rick?"

Pat had been standing at the corner of Bridge Street and Union Street, just next to Boots. The snow had not let up all day. It was deep even on the semi-cleared pavements. Cars were crawling and their headlights shone spooky moon yellow on the snowy roads. That top coat had been a good idea of Willie's. The second trip to Slaters in two days had been more expensive than the first. Man, Pat had thought to himself. He *needed* this job that Willie had set up for him just to pay him back.

"As I understand it, Rick, you've no discernible means of income. And yet, here you are, like a male model, in new clothes every time we see you?"

"Evening Mr B." Pat put out his hand and Grumphy actually smiled as he shook it. "How's Kylie?"

"She's fine. We're all going to try and keep it that way, son, eh?"

"I've not been called 'son' in a long time."

"Aye, well, its nae a term of endearment. I'm just reminding you fa's boss."

"That's very kind of you," said Pat, just about keeping his sarcasm under wraps, or so he thought.

"Don't mention it," replied Grumphy, doing the same.

Dod arrived too, he'd been talking on his phone, walking just behind Grumphy.

"Evening Pat."

"Evening Dod. Hang on, have you two been for a pint?"

"Aye, just a couple of quick eens,"said Grumphy.

"That's not fair. That means you've had time to compare notes." Pat was joking, trying to lighten the mood.

"Son, we've hud a nicht and a day tae compare notes."

"Yeah? And how'd I fair?"

"It could have been worse."

"High praise indeed."

"Oh, its nae praise. Its jist nae quite damnation, nae jist yet."

Pat blew on his hands and in an effort to get out of the north wind said, "So where are we off to, gents. I'm in your hands."

Grumphy and Dod looked at Pat. "You're shivering like a junkie, Rick. Dae they nae hae sna in Weeger?

Pat looked lost.

"Weeger?"

"*Glasgow,* if you want me tae say it proper, like."

"Mr B, where are we going?" Dod was anxious to ensure the initial exchanges were completed without gunfire.

"Just ower there. Come on. Poor Rick's gan to freeze till the spot."

Pat looked over the road and saw that Grumphy was marching onwards to Union Street with purpose and appeared to be heading straight to *Dreamy City*, which, under its flashing neon logo, had the words *Gentleman's Club* in lights. Pat looked at Dod, who looked back at him.

"Shall you tell him, or will I?" Pat had immediately grasped Grumphy's misunderstanding. Dod looked at Pat. "Tell him what?" And Dod started toward the Gentleman's Club too. Pat realised that they perhaps didn't have such clubs in Echt. He smiled to himself. This was going to lighten the mood no end – or at least lighten *his* mood.

Grumphy and Dod seemed deep in conversation which Pat, walking just behind them in the club after they'd entered, couldn't hear for the music. Pat had noticed that Dod and Grumphy were smelling of drink. A "couple o' quick eens" could mean anything from two to four pints.

The three of them were dressed very smartly and looked like businessmen, which was what everyone else looked like in the place. Pat wondered how long it would take for Grumphy to realise what kind of establishment they'd come into. There were girls wearing very little dancing on a small stage. Grumphy, Dod and Pat were shown to a table and they sat down. Grumphy got his coat off and was complaining about how stuffy it was. Pat was leaning over to try and hear properly while Dod was apparently "resting his eyes". Grumphy's speech was a bit slurred. He sat back, frustrated that Pat couldn't really hear what he was saying. All Pat had heard were some attempts to say something like "intentions" and "honourable". Grumphy sat back in his chair as Pat ordered drinks for the three of them. Brandies. The waitress went away to get their order and Pat went to say something to Grumphy but Grumphy was now "resting his eyes" too. Some 'bonding blether', thought Pat to himself as he surveyed the scene: one Echt loon sprawled on a chair and one elderly gentleman snoozing with his chin resting on his chest. Pat drank all three brandies when they arrived.

Pat wasn't sure how much time had passed when a topless dancer sauntered up to him, all seductive, or at least trying to be. This was not Pat's scene at all. She asked him if he wanted "a dance". Pat knew she meant some sleazy pseudo sexual writhing on his lap for money. Jeez. If he wanted sex, or even to pay for sex, there were more dignified ways of going about it. But just for a dance? What was that all about, he thought?

The girl was clearly getting nothing from Pat so she moved towards Dod but then moved away again as he was clearly an early casualty of a night out. Grumphy on the other hand simply looked as if he was examining his tie, as well he might, thought Pat, surmising that the tie had not seen the outside of a drawer in thirty years. So, the girl drifted over, dancing as she went, and leant down to speak to Grumphy. He near jumped out his skin as looked up, obviously having just been awoken from a deep doze. He wasn't all awake yet and the girl tried again to ask him something. He cocked his ear in her direction and she tried a third time. This time Pat heard what she said. "Would you like a dance?"

Grumphy looked totally put out as he'd been savouring his 40 winks but, being an old-fashioned gent of a certain age, he felt obliged to comply. So he replied loudly, "Aye, OK then," and stood up and started dancing as if it was some 1970s disco. He hadn't considered it pertinent that the lady asking him to dance, or so he thought, was naked except for pants. Slowly though, Grumphy's mind began to compute, and soon he was looking around realising that this lady was not alone in prowling around naked in the dark. He let out an involuntary, "fit the f***!" This was loud enough to startle even Dod, who looked up and saw a scene that he must have thought was a dream, but one that Kylie had better not catch him in. He shook himself like someone had thrown cold water over him. Bouncers were called as the old man with the 1970s tie was now considered a troublemaker. The girl was being shepherded away from the old man whose dancing had petrified her. Pat drained the last of the brandies on the table. But slowly. This scene was not going to be forgotten quickly. He wanted to capture every detail.

Two bouncers went to pick up Grumphy. Pat quickly went

over to explain that there was no problem and the old chap had just misunderstood. But the bouncers took issue partly because they relished a chance to actually earn the money they were paid and partly to look good to everyone at the same time. This was the kind of scene that bored Pat senseless as he'd seen it played a million times in bars all over the world. So he short circuited his debate with the bouncers by decking them both with one punch each. Patrons jumped up and screamed and shouted. More bouncers were coming on the scene. The two now unconscious bouncers were laid out, quite by chance, beside where Grumphy was standing. The new bouncers assumed Grumphy had knocked them out. This suited Pat, and now Dod, and they bopped the two new bouncers on the back of their heads and they too fell. Dod had a handy right hook, noticed Pat.

Pat quickly checked Grumphy was ok, and he replied as if it was a daft question. Daft or not, it was time to get out and thanks in part to the confusion and in part to the sheer size of Dod, they managed to leave unhindered.

Soon they found themselves slinking off Union Street and into Golden Square. Dod, now feeling terrible guilt over his reaction in the Gentleman's Club, was certain that every police siren was from a car seeking him out. Pat thought it prudent to not be too visible on the main drag just in case the bouncers were looking for them. Grumphy was outraged that the club had miss-sold itself to him, or so he believed. "They had it coming," was all he said.

They found another pub, the Globe and they piled in.

"Where'd you pick up that right hook, Dod? Came in pretty handy," asked Pat.

"Rugby."

Grumphy nodded, impressed. There might be more to

rugby than he'd supposed. He then put his hand out to Pat. "Well, I've no choice but to offer you my thanks, Pat."

"'Pat'? I'm honoured."

Grumphy laughed, then added, "Aye, you are. Dinna forget it."

Pat shook his hand. "

"You too, Dod. I might yet mak a trip to Murrayfield in your honour."

"I'm really sorry Mr B. I don't know what came over me."

"Instinct, Dod," said Pat. "As long as you don't make a habit of it, it's not a bad instinct." He turned to Grumphy. "Mr B, how did you find that club?"

"Bloody internet. That's the last time I'm going on the web to find onyhin."

"I dunno," said Pat, "You were quite a mover. I think that girl was into you."

"Ha ha," Grumphy laughed, adding, "it's this tie. The ladies love this tie."

"Ha ha." Dod was now relaxing after the excitement. "Maybe you'd get a job there, Mr B, dancing on the tables."

"Jesus. Don't, Dod, in the name of God, don't."

Against the odds, Grumphy and Pat got on so well that Dod's whatever refereeing skills Kylie hoped Dod might have were not needed. Describing Pat and Grumphy as 'Blood brothers' might have exaggerated this new-found Détente but the end of this particular Cold War looked like it might be in sight.

They talked fitba, about the Dons. They even talked rugby, or rather listened to Dod talk about it. They talked about earlier events in the evening and about previous brushes with the law, or even with their own consciences. Pat confessed to "schooshing" most pedestrians that ever walked Union

103

Street in the mid-1980s, using the window washers on the windscreen of whatever car his sales team were in at the time. Grumphy confessed to making a crank call as a joke to a mate which had backfired spectacularly when said mate had a heart attack as he shouted at what he thought were the Dutch police who, he thought, wanted to interview him about his smuggling hash into the UK. Grumphy had heard that said mate had done this and so hence the wind-up call. Said mate lived to tell the tale but never knew who the culprit was. In fact, he'd told Grumphy that he'd "skin" whoever had done it with a "blunt axe". Grumphy had nodded, agreeing with every word and making a mental note to "bid awa fae that loon fur a whilie." Dod confessed that he's once stolen all the golf balls from Codona's at the beach. As if that wasn't a tame enough confession, he further confessed that he'd put them all back the next day, at which Grumphy and Pat had groaned loudly.

Dod practically carried Grumphy up Skene Street and Esslemont Avenue, but not before the three of them had encountered a snowman someone had taken the trouble to build on Union Terrace. Whoever had made it had even somehow found a carrot to use as a nose, two apples as eyes and a banana as a mouth. There were a few restaurants nearby so Grumphy had speculated that bored staff must have created the snowman.

"Pat, what are you doing?" asked Grumphy as Pat staggered over to the snowman, sniggering. Dod was leaning against a wall, trying to focus on the screen of his phone, hoping he didn't have to call Kylie back if she'd called because he was slurring even in his own head, never mind out loud.

Pat was, according to Grumphy, "steamin'". Pat had reached the snowman and Grumphy wondered if he'd try and speak to it. Grumphy was giggling at the thought.

"Hey, Grumphy," called Pat, "Watch this."

"I'll 'Grumphy' ye. Now, Pat, leave that poor snowman alone." He turned to Dod, saying, "Dod, turn awa, loon, I think he's gan to abuse the snowman."

Grumphy needn't have worried. The chances of Dod focusing on anything were slim.

Pat on the other hand was focused intently on the snow-man but Grumphy couldn't see what he was doing until Pat stepped back, shouting, "Voilà!" and pointing to the snowman, whose carrot nose and apple eyes had been trans-planted from the poor thing's head to its genital area so that it now had a carrot manhood and apple testicles, although it still had its banana smile. Pat was now holding himself up against a granite wall as he laughed himself unsteady. Grumphy looked at the scene a little disapprovingly, until he heard Dod suddenly howl with laughter. Grumphy looked round. Dod was pointing at the mutilated snowman, laugh-ing hysterically. Seeing the other two like this was infectious and soon Grumphy too was belly aching with laughter.

A middle-aged couple passed them by and loudly tutted as the three smartly dressed men held themselves up against a wall while pointing at the snowman.

"C'mon, yoos. We're embarrassing ourselves. Sober up, troops." Grumphy was trying to assume some kind of authority. Dod appeared to be sobering up a bit. Pat wasn't that drunk. His month "on leave" in Glasgow had been good training for missions like this.

"Mon, Dod, we've Esslemont to walk up yet."

Dod still had traces of laughter oozing out of him as he and Pat hugged like drunks. "Grumphy couldn't resist a joke at the Weegie's expense. "He'll have your wallet by now, Dod. Get up here while you've still got the shirt on your back."

"Dod, you're a good fella," said Pat. "I've not just found a daughter. I've found a son in law too."

"You're not so bad yourself, Rick," said Dod, still giggling.

"Grumphy called over. "It's OK, Dod, we can call him 'Pat' now. I think he's earned a reprieve, for now, onywy."

"Congratulations! You're 'Pat'! said Dod.

Pat looked over at Grumphy. Grumphy said, "Ach, I suppose another handshake is in order. But dinna steal my watch." Pat and he shook hands warmly. "The funny thing is, Pat, Kylie needs a dad. Despite me being an obviously fine physical specimen, I'll nae be aroon forever."

Pat laughed and said, "So, I'm on the sub's bench?"

"Grumphy, looked at him and smiled. "Aye, you might jist get a game yet, son. Stick in at it, though."

Pat laughed. Grumphy took his hand and shook it again, but added, "I mean it, Pat."

Pat looked back at him. "I will, George. I promise you."

"Da promise me. Just dae it."

Pat nodded.

"By the way, your nae oot the woods yet.

Pat looked questioningly at Grumphy, who said, "You've still got The Summerhill Mob to meet."

Stick and Carrot

Mither wasn't in the mood for Grumphy's hangover. Truth be told, neither was Grumphy. She'd just walked back from the Trinity Centre over icy pavements which had soured her mood somewhat. In addition, she'd tutted on the way along Union Terrace because some young loons, she supposed, had done rude things to a snowman which, although melting, still managed to look obscene. "Someone should move that carrot, for goodness sake," she'd said to herself, doubtless echoing the thoughts of all decent-minded citizens who'd spotted the scene. She'd told Grumphy this while he was sitting at the table with a strong cuppy and his head in his hands. He didn't look well, and she could've sworn she'd seen him shake a little, when she'd told him about the snowman and the carrot. The DTs, eh? He must be really suffering today, she'd thought.

Pat had managed to make it to breakfast at his hotel, usually a highlight of the day. But today he was more thirsty than hungry. Numerous cups of tea helped him attain something approaching sobriety, which was a wee bonus considering he had an interview at 11am.

Dod had slept on the settee at Esslemont Avenue, been woken by – and shouted at – by Kylie and had reluctantly been dragged to Union Square to look at goodness knew what. To make matters worse, Kylie insisted on walking. He understood that this was punishment. They too had walked passed the snowman and his dangly carrot. However, Dod had no memory of the night before, which became a source of frustration to Kylie who asked repeatedly how the night had gone. It'd taken a discreet call to Grumphy, while Kylie looked at wifie clothes, to get the basics. These he imparted to Kylie and she was pleased that it had passed off not only peacefully but actually very well. At least, that's how it sounded from Dod's abstract fragments of memory.

Pat, as it happened was passing through Union Square on his way to Admiral Court for his interview around the same time. He noticed a text from Dod, saying he was at Union Square and Kylie was asking what had happened the night before and, as he didn't know, any clues would be helpful. Pat called him. He was with Kylie at Patisserie Valerie drinking a well-earned coffee. Kylie took the phone and almost called Pat "Dad" but stopped herself. But "father" sounded too formal. And "Pat", well, you didn't call your father by his name. So she ended up saying, "Fit like."

"I'm fine, Kylie."

"Join us for coffee seeing as you are here."

He saw them sitting at an outside table and he joined them.

"An interview?" said Kylie. "So, you're hanging around?"

"That I am."

"Good."

"What else could I do? I've got a wedding to prepare for," said Pat, smiling.

Kylie felt so very comfortable with this stranger she'd only met two days ago and who happened to be her father. She felt immense gratitude to Dod. He really knew what she needed. "So, when are we seeing you again?"

"Whenever you want, Kylie. Or whenever Dod lets you out."

"Da worry aboot that!"

They all laughed.

"So, 'Faither', I hear you're being called in front of the Summerhill Mob?"

Pat quite liked being called, "Faither". Obviously it was a compromise between "Father" and "Dad". Little steps.

"Word gets around in a small town," said Pat, on a slight Glasgow versus Aberdeen wind-up.

"They're not so bad, Pat. They seem to have accepted me ok," said Dod.

"That's what you think, honey," said Kylie, with a mischievous smile.

"You're not tainted with Weegieness though, Dod," said Pat.

"That's true," said Dod, with his own sense of humour fighting its way through his hangover.

"So, Faither, fits the job you're going for?"

Pat filled her in, and told her more about his time in the army. There was so much to tell her. And there was so much he wanted to know. Kylie told him about Uni, about why she wanted to teach, about how she loved Aberdeen, about how she and Dod met. And there was still whole lifetimes to discuss. But for now, Pat had to make tracks to his job Interview.

"Ma said she was going to take us up to Aunt Jessie's and Uncle James's for supper tomorrow night."

"Mmm, Jessie James? Let me guess. The Summerhill Mob."

Kylie pointed a finger at him and pulled an imaginary trigger, saying, "got it in one, Faither."

So, that was settled. Pat set off to Admiral Court and made it in time, just. But he was on a cloud. For the first time in a few years he felt that life was good and could get even better. He sat in reception until a man called Graham came downstairs to greet him and take him up to the offices of *Gregson Engineering*. There, in an office with Graham and two other chaps, Kyle, and Andrew, Pat discussed his time in the army, answering questions which seemed fixated on his time in Iraq. These guys wanted war stories, thought Pat. They spoke posh and talked very slow and deliberately, like everything they said was vitally important. They sounded like off-duty Ruperts, except even Ruperts didn't ask soldiers about war just for cheap thrills. Think Kylie, think money, think anything other than walking out.

"So, Willie told us you're a golfer. Always helps. Always more comfortable employing chaps we can discuss things with on the course. I'm told you've joined a club here?"

Pat, knew he had to be what they wanted him to be. He was remembering Willie's advice. It was time to method act. He mentally got into character. He was a golfer. He lived and breathed golf. He'd only had a short time to surf the web and research golfing terms and facts. But he knew this discussion would not be in-depth. Just need a few morsels to give to these clowns, thought Pat. Pat had been adopting their mannerisms, and imitating their hypnotically slow pace of speech too.

"So, where do you play?"

Shit. He had some golf terms, some golf facts, but he didn't know *any* golf club in Aberdeen. Wait, what was it Dod had said when they were out last night? Something about stealing golf balls? That must have been from a golf course. That'll do. Pat looked at them, sitting with his legs crossed, just like they all were sitting, and said, slowly and deliberately, "Codona's."

There was silence in the room. Pat was sure he could hear something like a clock ticking, but it might just have been the time bomb ticking on his career. Pat didn't say a word. He didn't know what word to say. They'd have had looked less stunned, Pat thought, if he'd had stood up, dropped his kegs, and done a jobby on the carpet. After what seemed ages, the Graham chap burst out laughing. Then the Kyle and Andrew chaps did too. In fact they seemed genuinely amused. Pat just smiled. Eventually, the Graham chap said, "Brilliant. Absolutely brilliant. We *love* dead-pan humour."

The Andrew chap added, "Yes, bravo. You had us going there, I think. Very funny indeed."

Pat made a mental note. Codona's probably wasn't the number one golfing destination in this part of world. Pat would later learn that Codona's was a funfair with only a crazy golf area and he'd cringe with embarrassment at his error. Whereas the chaps in the office had thought he'd made a very witty remark.

"Well, Pat, if you ever fancy a round at my club, just let me know. It'd be my pleasure." The Graham chap seemed to be head chap. The other chaps offered Pat rounds of golf too. Clearly, Pat was a hit, although he couldn't really work out why.

Clocked

Willie was bang on time as always. He was very keen to hear how Pat had gotten on at the interview the day before. He already knew Pat had got the job. But he was still keen to hear it in Pat's own words.

Pat was only minutes later. He'd had to ask someone where exactly *The Contour Café*, on The Green, was. So, here they were, standing in the small queue for mid-morning coffee. Willie had a great big smile on his face and was dying to say something to Pat. Pat ordered his usual tea and Willie his Americano. They sat down, Willie still looking at Pat, grinning.

"What?"

Willie could wait no more.

"Codona's! Ahahahah!!!"

"How was I to know?"

Willie eventually composed himself.

"God knows how you got the job."

"Perhaps because they were as thick as planks?"

"At least you wouldn't expect them to turn up at Codona's with golf bag, caddy and a golf cart!"

Pat laughed a little. "They think I'm a funny guy."

"Ha ha! Pat! You are a funny guy!"

"Are you sure they thought I was joking?"

Willie looked out the window, wanting Pat to stew a bit, just for fun. Then he looked back at him and said, "Aye. They thought you were joking. Thank God. But the truth is you already had passed the interview before you got there."

"How come?"

Willie smiled and then said, "Sounds like you had quite a night out with Grumphy and Dod?"

"Did you speak to them?"

"No."

"But, you and I didn't speak yesterday?"

Willie smiled again. "I know."

Pat looked at him. "So . . . ?"

"Do you remember when I did your CV for you?"

"Yeah?"

"And I got you to take a photograph to put on it?"

"Yes, what a pointless thing that is. A photo on a CV. As if how you look would affect a job interview."

"Well, sometimes it might. Anyway, people like to know who they are dealing with and a visual helps."

"Okay, so, what's your point?"

"Tell me about your night out first. I've not heard about it yet. Well, not from you anyway."

Pat looked stumped. Willie had obviously heard something about the wild night out. But from who?

"Let's just say you did your application to become head of Security no harm by laying out a few bouncers. In fact, you might want to make Dod your number two, from what I hear."

"Spill it, Willie."

"Let's just say that a certain chap, by name of Andrew, happened to be in a certain Gentleman's Club in town the other night and was treated to a bit of a boxing show."

Pat sat back, a bit stunned. But, then again, when considering the Andrew chap, it wasn't all that surprising at all. He seemed dim enough to go to places like that.

"The poor lassies in these places. God, I'd hate it if that was my daughter."

"Well, let's leave your moralising out of any chats you have with Andrew, until you have a wee wedge in the bank. Then you can tell him whatever you like."

Pat thought about it, then said, "Impressed, was he?"

"Ooo, yes. These chaps like a bit of roughness. Makes them feel like they're living life on the edge, rather than just on the edge of a leather chair. He'll be dining out on that story for years."

"So, I got the job you say?"

"Aye."

"When do I start?"

"Monday."

"Monday? That's quick!"

"You've already had a month off, so what are you moaning about."

"Well, I just wanted to spend a bit more time with Kylie."

"You spent time with her now, without pennies, or, you can do what the rest of us do and fit your social life around a job?"

"Aye, okay."

"Pat, this is a real job. With real money. Andrew will call you tonight. Act like you didn't already know you got the job."

"Gotcha."

The Summerhill Mob

Pat hadn't really been nervous for his job interview. Everything was happening so quickly he hardly had time to catch his breath. But now, in Grumphy's car, heading along Lang Stracht to Summerhill, he felt a bit more apprehensive. He'd never met them before when he was dating Dorothy in the 1980s. But he'd heard about them. Decent, hard-working and hardy folks who didn't take any shit and who looked after the most important thing in life. Family. This was Grumphy's two brothers and their families. Grumphy was the oldest of them but there was, from what Pat heard, constant competition to be head of the family.

There was James. 68 and a retired spark. Married for 40 years to Mags, with three sons. Two had been in the army. A good sign as far as Pat was concerned. One was in the police.

Then there was Freddie, 66, and his son and daughter. Freddie and his wife, Angie, had run their own café in Torry for years until he'd retired last year.

All of them were Aberdeen FC fans and all had season tickets.

All of them had a special place in their hearts for Dorothy, and therefore for Kylie too. Dorothy had made her way in the world on her own and brought up Kylie, who James had once called The Whiny Quinie when she was four as she had been quite determined to get an extra ice cream at Aberdeen beach once summer day when they were all there. The nickname had stuck and although it wasn't used often now that Kylie was grown up, James and others reserved the right the use it whenever they liked. Kylie had given up asking them not to as any such request was invariably met with extra usage of the nick name. Besides, it was said with affection. Dorothy and Kylie were considered as close as anyone to the fiercely protective Summerhill Mob.

This was the den Pat was walking, Daniel-like, into. Although it had only been four days since Pat's return, every scrap of information on him had been fed through the Summerhill Mob's system. They knew where he was staying, who he'd met, where he'd been, and where he was going. They heard everything about the job interview, which had pleased them, and everything about The Gentlemen's Club, which hadn't pleased them. But, they blamed that a little on Grumphy, even if they wouldn't say that out loud. They weren't quite sure why Pat had left the army, but, as two of them were military men, they had worked out that it wasn't exactly voluntarily.

Grumphy pulled up at James's house, a former council property which James had bought years ago and which he and his pals had renovated and made it into what Grumphy called Summerhill Palace.

After the polite introductions had been made, Pat found himself sitting next to Dorothy and opposite Kylie and Dod. Dod seemed warmly welcomed, thought Pat. He must have passed all the tests, Grumphy sat beside Mither at the top of the table.

Supper had been served and Pat had been nervously making conversation with the relatives and they'd been much less frosty than he'd expected. But there was obviously a distance of sorts. The few chances he'd had to chat to Dorothy had been productive, thought Pat, as Dorothy had been almost warmly responding. The fact that they had a daughter

116

in common, and who was sitting right across from them, made Pat and Dorothy feel a lot closer than they'd perhaps expected to feel. They'd caught each other's eyes a few times and shared a decent wee laugh or two. They watched what Kylie called "The Mither and Grumphy Show" unfold at the top of the table. Both Pat and Dorothy caught the nuances of that relationship and they exchanged smiles several times, mostly when Mither was chiding Grumphy about something, and he was adopting something of an anti-chiding stance. It was like a dance, him about to do or say something but then checking back to see if Mither approved or not, then him guessing that she did but guessing wrongly and then him doing his "off camera" look of frustration when Mither expressed her disapproval. Pat looked around the table and it seemed that he, Dorothy and Kylie were the ones most amused by this. He felt very close to Kylie and he knew that this was luck very few people had. Strangely, he felt immense warmth towards Dorothy too. She was the mother of his newly discovered prize possession. She had given him this. Later than perhaps she should have done. But late or not, she had given him the greatest gift a man could have. As the chat progressed and the tea and water flowed (no alcohol was allowed in this house, Pat had learned), everyone seemed to be coming gelled together with chat, the sharing of anecdotes no one outside the group could ever see humour in, with laughter, with warmth, with the exchanging of dozens of little looks, glances, smiles, with various kindnesses, and with a few of the hands holding other hands both over and under the table, and with love.

Grumphy had been speaking away to James at the top of the table, and Freddie had stood up to join in with whatever they were saying. Pat couldn't hear what was being said as everyone was speaking at the same time to everyone, or so it seemed to Pat. He thought back to that lonely month in Glasgow, in Willie's flat. He'd despaired every day that started. Only he never admitted that to himself. He admitted it now, silently to himself. He also admitted how hard it had been to be effectively thrown out the army but also he admitted now that, had he been still loving the army then he wouldn't have ever "bopped a Rupert". The army had seemed real life. But it hadn't been. It now seemed a long-term illusion. Looking around him at this moment he saw something he hadn't really seen ever in adulthood. Real life. Real family. It wasn't his family, or at least it wasn't all his family, at least, it wasn't yet. But, my God, he thought, listen to this. The sounds of everyone speaking, shouting, laughing, cackling, nipping, shoving, sharing – it sounded like the most beautiful morning birdsong he'd ever heard. Perhaps this was the birdsong that he'd been hearing all these years.

Fitever! is just the first in a series of books following the trials and tribulations of Mither and Grumphy, The Whiny Quinie, The Summerhill Mob, and of course, Pat and Dorothy.

The second book is *Wise Up!* published in July 2016 and *Canna Winna Dinna,* published in November 2016.

Look out too for the Fitever! website coming in June and who knows, Grumphy might even take to Twitter, because, as readers of Fitever! know, Grumphy love's technology:)